MONSTER HUNTER FOR HIRE

SUPERNATURAL SOLUTIONS

THE MARC TEMPLE CASEFILES - VOLUME 1

DEREK M. KOCH

EXPERIENCED PROFESSIONAL AVAILABLE NOW TO RID YOU OF YOUR SUPERNATURAL, GHOULISH, AND MONSTER PESTS. WILL COME TO YOUR HOME OR BUSINESS. DISCREET. PRICES VARY.

CONTENTS

WHO IS MARC TEMPLE?

As a character, Marc Temple's first appearance on the page happened in 2010. At the time, I was producing the Mail Order Zombie podcast, and as one might be able to tell from the name of the show, it was about zombies. Back then, I was obsessed with zombie media, and when I was approached to join a loose collective of other horror-centric podcasters and contribute to an anthology, I dusted off something I started writing a few years prior, completed it, and sent it in.

The short story "The Law" appeared in Apparatus Revolution's anthology *Dark: A Horror Anthology* in September of that year.

Marc later appeared in 2011. The short story "2-For-1 Chinese Special" was included in the (now out-of-print) anthology *Leather, Denim & Silver: Legends of the Monster Hunter* from Pill Hill Press.

I don't know if I'd consider these two stories canon to who and what Marc Temple is today, and obviously my writing style has evolved somewhat over the years. However, for completists, I've included these two short stories, relatively unedited, at the end of this book.

"The Law" started as a writing exercise, and "2-For-1 Chinese Special" came from a desire to revisit the lone monster hunter working in the private sector as an exterminator. However, the seeds of Marc Temple were planted in the late-90s when, I, along with a small cast and crew of friends, shot a short movie called "Cash Only" (we thought we were clever when we wrote the title as "Ca$h Only" whenever referring to the short movie online). This short movie featured a monster hunter named Drake (the name inspired, no doubt, by the Marvel Comics' character Frank Drake) who receives a call from a bar owner dealing with a pesky undead pest situation. She hires Drake to come to her bar, and George A. Romero-style, Drake dispatches the zombies with headshots. However, due to Drake's strange bullet economy (he only brought six bullets because the bar owner only reported six zombies), he's surprised when he finds more zombies than bargained for. Ultimately, Drake doesn't eliminate all the zombies, but he does manage to walk away from the encounter, even if the bar owner doesn't.

I never did anything else with this Drake character, but the idea of a man hiring himself out to deal with threats of a supernatural nature stuck with me. That idea eventually became Marc Temple.

As I continued to write Marc Temple stories, the world around him continued to take shape. These tales exist in our world, the real world . . . if there were such things as vampires, werewolves, zombies, ghouls, and all the rest.

Although, it's not for me to say there aren't such things. I mean, I've not SEEN any in person myself, but that might just be because Marc Temple is really good at his job.

- Derek M. Koch, 2019

HIGH STAKES

Marc Temple didn't like to travel unarmed, but sometimes he didn't have a choice. He fidgeted in his seat and stretched one of his legs out into the aisle, but pulled it back when one of the attendants glared at him.

He hated flying.

Especially when his client didn't pop for first class.

The seat belt light was still on, and Marc was already sweating. He guessed he'd been in the air for less than fifteen minutes, but he wanted to stand and stretch. The air conditioning wasn't working, so he twisted in his seat to work his leather jacket free.

Someone's child started screaming.

Marc closed his eyes and focused on the job at hand.

The flight was full, which Marc thought was odd for such a late flight. Not only did that make him uncomfortable, but it would make his job more difficult. Not that he ever let himself think destroying a vampire was easy, but to do so on a full airplane in mid-flight seemed a near-impossible task.

But that's what his client paid him to do.

When she contacted Marc two weeks ago, she tried to tell him why she wanted this particular vampire killed. Marc didn't need to know. He didn't want to know. Marc was an elimination and extermination specialist, and didn't want to hear about how this vampire had worked his way into the business world and ended up working for a rival PR company. Marc didn't care that his client lost several accounts, and that she blamed this particular vampire. All he cared about was trying to find a way to finish the job before they landed.

He glanced to his side. His row was three narrow seats wide, and the college student in the middle seat was doing his best to keep from touching anyone else. He kept his head down, his eyes focused on the open Sudoku puzzle book in his lap.

Past him, in the window seat, sat an older man with gray hair and a darker gray suit. His head was turned toward the window, but Marc knew what his face looked like. The client sent him several photos of the target when Marc took the job.

Marc looked up when the seat belt light sounded. He let a heavy sigh slip as he stretched his leg out again. The flight attendant didn't scowl at him this time. He was grateful. He didn't want to draw too much attention.

"Excuse me."

Marc turned his head to see a woman standing in the aisle behind him. She didn't make eye contact with him. She only stared at his outstretched leg.

"Sorry." Marc pulled back his leg to let the woman pass. He watched her continue down the aisle and disappear in the airplane's bathroom.

Marc knew he needed to get himself to the bathroom soon, and tried not to be too upset that he wasn't the first one in there. He stretched again and waited.

He would have taken a train to Phoenix if this job didn't land in his lap. He had business in Arizona, and preferred to travel by rail. He hated feeling so vulnerable in the air. Too many variables. Not enough weapons. Not normally worth the expense.

But a paycheck was a paycheck, and this paycheck had more zeros on it than Marc had seen in a while.

He casually glanced at the other passengers in his row. The college student turned a page in his puzzle book. The vampire kept staring out the window. Marc noted the vampire held his head in such a way as not to reveal that his face didn't cast a reflection in the small window.

Not that Marc needed confirmation. As much as he hated doing it, he used one of his few remaining contacts at the Bureau to get a ticket with his name on it as close to his target as possible.

This was supposed to be a short flight, but he never trusted the arrival times. Traveling by train wasn't much better, but a train wasn't as likely to be rerouted or to lose his luggage. The air wasn't as stale. The other passengers weren't as crammed next to him. If there was a screaming child, either he or the parents - after enough appropriate scowls from Marc - could move. On a plane, he was too restricted, and that made it hard for him to feel prepared for the job at hand.

Marc looked to the bathroom, and waited for the door to open. When it finally did, Marc started to stand, and made it clear to any other passenger that might have been waiting that he was next. He let the woman pass, and made for the bathroom himself, checking that the permanent marker he brought onto the plane with him was still tucked in his back pocket.

Marc slid the Sharpie back into his pants as he left the lavatory. It wasn't hard to disable the lock, and prepping the rest of the bathroom for what he had in mind didn't take too long. And since he managed to get close enough to the potable water when he boarded the plane with the other passengers earlier, he didn't have anything else to do at this point but to wait.

He got back to his seat, leaned back in his chair, and closed his eyes.

Marc didn't let himself fall asleep, so he heard the flight attendant when she started rolling the service cart down the aisle. He opened his eyes, straightened, and pulled in his leg to make room for her to pass. The college student sitting next to him closed his puzzle book and looked expectantly to the flight attendant. Marc swore he saw the kid lick his lips, but Marc wasn't trying to pay attention to him.

His focus was on the vampire.

The PR man Marc had been hired to prevent from ever leaving this plane intact stared forward, his cold eyes dead ahead at the approaching flight attendant. Marc didn't look directly at the man, but kept him in his peripheral vision. The vampire seemed interested in the refreshments the attendants were handing out to the passengers. Marc nodded to himself.

This was going to work. Marc let a slight smile settle on his lips.

He continued to smile when the attendant reached his row.

"Something to drink?"

Marc answered casually. "Sure. Water."

"And you, sir?"

The college kid nodded. "Coke."

"And, sir?"

Marc slid his eyes to side to watch for the vampire's response.

"Do you have coffee?"

"We can make some, sir. Sugar? Cream?"

"Black."

Marc held back an even wider grin. As long as the coffee was made with the same water he blessed earlier, this was going to work.

The flight attendant told the vampire she'd be back with his coffee.

The vampire nodded.

Marc waited.

He took his plastic cup of water from the attendant, and leaned out of her way when we she passed a cup to Sudoku Boy, but took the opportunity to slide the kid's pencil off his tray. Marc tucked the no. 2 beneath one of his legs as he watched the flight attendant pour a cup of coffee for the vampire.

Marc waited.

And hoped the vampire liked to drink his coffee hot. He wanted this job to be over soon.

He wasn't expecting to find a wooden pencil on the airplane, and he feigned ignorance when the college kid started looking for it. Irritated disinterest colored the vampire's face as the kid squirmed in his seat. Eventually, he gave up and found a pen in his shirt pocket before going back to his Sudoku.

As the flight attendant moved to another row, Marc sipped his water. It tasted fine to him.

And at first, the vampire gave no indication anything was wrong with his beverage either. Marc drained his water with a few gulps, and continued to watch.

It took almost too long.

Almost.

The vampire's body stiffened. He grabbed for his arm rest, but missed and latched onto the college student's arm instead. The kid looked uncomfortable at first, and tried to pull away, but when the vampire refused to let go, Sudoku Boy started to panic.

Marc braced himself for the scene a screaming college kid on a crowded airplane would make, but the vampire suddenly went limp. The college student yanked his arm away, and opened his mouth to say something, but when he didn't, Marc shifted his attention to his target.

The vampire was staring into the student's eyes.

Marc knew the holy water in the coffee would weaken the vampire, but he was glad it didn't weaken him so much that he couldn't mesmerize someone. He didn't need a scene.

The college student's face went slack as the vampire struggled to get out of his seat. Marc stood and stepped into the aisle, all the while watching the other passengers and flight attendants.

They hadn't drawn too much attention.

Hopefully it would stay that way.

The vampire clutched his stomach and struggled to stand once he freed himself from their row. Marc stepped back and placed a hand on his shoulder before leaning close to his target. "Are you feeling all right?"

The vampire's eyes locked onto Marc's. Marc fought the temptation to shudder. He'd lost track of how many vampires he'd destroyed over the years, but every time he made eye contact with one, it still shook him. He learned a long time ago how to turn the fear normally associated with locking eyes with a one of these things into rage, but even now, this vampire wanted something of Marc when he gazed at him.

He felt himself falling into the weakened vampire's eyes. Marc worked against their pull, mentally swimming against the tide threatening to drag his will into the vampire's mind. He fought . . .

Marc slowly nodded, offered the vampire his shoulder, and steered him toward the bathroom.

He struggled to keep control. Marc tried not to gasp as the vampire lessened its mental grip on him when a flight attendant approached them.

The attendant opened her mouth to speak, but her jaw tightened and she clamped her mouth shut. Marc felt the connection the vampire was trying to make with him loosen. He assumed the monster had turned his attention to the attendant.

Marc hadn't counted on the vampire helping to get them to the bathroom, but he wasn't going to turn down the assist.

The flight attendant's knees wavered, and she steadied herself on the back of one of the seats. Marc and the vampire moved around her. It was a tight fit, and Marc sought her eyes as she held herself up.

She wouldn't stop them. The vampire shut her down. She'd be lucky to remember even coming to work today.

One less person to remember two people walking to the bathroom, when - if Marc had anything to say about it - only one person would walk out.

No one else tried to stop them as they continued on their way. Marc felt the vampire trying to connect with his thoughts again, so he played along. He assumed the vampire intended to feed on him in the airplane's lavatory. The research he'd done on the creature told him this vampire liked to keep a low profile, and feeding in private matched his MO. If the vampire wanted to make a quick snack out of Marc to heal any damage done by drinking the holy water coffee brew, Marc wasn't going to try to stop him.

Yet.

Once they didn't have any witnesses, though, Marc had no intention of playing along anymore.

They reached the bathroom. Marc quickly looked back. The flight attendant that had approached them before was back to doing her job. She ignored Marc, even when she made eye contact with him.

Marc hated having so many variables when it came to doing a job, but sometimes these happy accidents came along, and he wasn't going to complain. All his client would know is that Marc finished the job. He wouldn't even charge extra for any complications.

As long as the rest of this went well.

The vampire opened the bathroom door and slunk inside. Marc squeezed in behind and pulled the door shut behind them.

There wasn't a lot of space for two grown men inside the bathroom, which worked to Marc's benefit. It meant the vampire couldn't get too far away from any of the crosses Marc had drawn around the room earlier with his Sharpie.

He felt the vampire's attempted mesmerism drop. Marc maneuvered behind the vampire and pressed his back against the door. He expected his target to scream, make some sort of noise, and braced himself accordingly. As much as he appreciated what such a sound signified, he hated the sound of a vampire in distress.

The vampire pinballed between the confining walls, avoiding the Sharpie crosses as best he could, but every time his shoulder, his back, or his knees came into contact with one, which was often considering the confines of an airplane bathroom, the vampire shrieked and bounced away. Marc shoved himself into an awkward corner to avoid the vampire when the monster reached for him. He felt cold tendrils reaching from the vampire's mind to his own for help, but Marc shook them off. He let the anger he felt toward these undead creatures shield him as he watched the vampire come to rest in a small heap in the near center of the bathroom.

Marc had to squeeze around him to find an opening. When he moved away from the door, the vampire's arm shot out, reaching for the doorknob. It sizzled when it made contact with the small cross Marc had drawn on it earlier. For a moment, Marc thought it would succeed in twisting the doorknob anyway, but he shouldn't have worried.

The monster was too weak.

As the vampire let its arm drop, Marc slipped the Sudoku kid's pencil out of his pocket with one hand. With his other, he bent the vampire over the small sink.

The vampire hissed.

Marc slammed the wooden pencil into its back.

He felt the tip of it break as it pushed between the vampire's ribs, but the rest of the pencil held as he pressed it into the vampire's undead heart.

When it was done, Marc rinsed what remained of the vampire down the sink. He flushed the larger pieces. Of course, he blessed the water he used to clean up for insurance. He was fortunate he didn't get much gore on himself. He wouldn't need to add a dry-cleaning charge to his client's final bill.

He let himself out of the bathroom. No one was waiting for him. Marc was glad this vampire's charm lingered after its destruction. The flight attendant that approached them earlier all but ignored him as he made his way back to his seat.

The college student didn't look up. He was focused on his Sudoku again. Marc hated to thank a vampire for anything, but since the vampire assisted in making its own death as inconspicuous as possible, he thanked it anyway.

A woman four rows down on the other side of the aisle screamed. She jumped to her feet, still holding her plastic cup of water. A flight attendant - not the one earlier mesmerized - walked quickly to her while other passengers either tried to get away form her.

Marc guessed the woman was maybe in her forties. She wore a tight-fitting black top with spaghetti straps, too much hairspray, and a look of disgust on her face. She coughed, and frothy blood splattered from her lips. She threw the cup of water at the approaching flight attendant and collapsed back in her seat.

Marc didn't expect there to be a second vampire on the plane. He looked around, hoping to find a weapon of some sort in case it regained consciousness.

But she didn't.

HALFWAY TO IDAHO

"Do you have a cell phone? Hey, mister! Do you have a phone?"

Marc Temple heard her, but he kept his attention on the blood trail that seemed to pulse in the emergency lights. His eyes tracked the smeared blood skittering from the front of the woman's Honda, crossing both lanes of the two-lane highway, and disappearing in the trees that themselves seemed to disappear in the night.

"He's bleeding! Dammit, do you have a phone?"

Marc shook his head, but kept his eyes on the trees. "I already tried to call someone. No signal."

Squinting didn't make it any easier for him to see in the dark, but Marc squinted anyway. The trees refused to give up any secrets. Marc finally looked back at the couple huddled in front of the Honda. He didn't need this right now. He could have kept driving. He had a client waiting for him in Pocatello, and he hated missing appointments. But when he came across the Honda squatting on the side of the road ten minutes ago, he knew he needed to at least stop to see if there was anything he could do. Especially when he considered the amount of blood shining back at him in the moonlight.

Marc sighed and stepped around to the front of the Honda. The woman - a twenty-something with blood streaked across her temples from where she kept running her hands through her blonde hair - squatted in front of a man - probably the same age and not moving - who sat propped against the front of the car. "Is he breathing?"

The woman didn't look at Marc as she answered. "Yes, but he won't open his eyes."

"Let me take a look." Marc moved to her side and placed a hand on her shoulder. "What's his name?"

"MJ."

"And what's yours?"

She pulled her eyes away from MJ and looked at Marc as she stood. "Brandi."

"Okay. Brandi. I'm Marc, and I'm going to take a look at MJ. Okay?"

Brandi nodded. "I think he's still breathing."

"Go watch for any oncoming traffic. If anyone drives by, flag them down."

"Okay."

Marc knelt in front of MJ as Brandi stepped across the street. He didn't need this. But neither did MJ or Brandi. "MJ? Can you hear me?" Marc nudged MJ's chin up and tilted his still head from side to side. Brandi was right. He was breathing, but he wasn't responding. And she was also right about his bleeding. Marc let MJ's head rest before focusing on his arm. He wore a red windbreaker, and something had torn a baseball-sized hole in his left sleeve. Marc pulled the edges of the torn jacket back to see bloody rips in his flesh just as jagged.

He looked up at Brandi. She stood in the middle of the road, slowly turning in small circles to watch for traffic coming from either direction. Marc didn't have any flares, so he hoped both cars' emergency flashers and the moonlight would give any unlikely drivers enough light to keep from hitting her. He called to her. "Anything?"

Brandi stopped turning. "I don't see anyone." Marc stood and moved to the driver's side of the Honda. He saw a backpack and a messenger bag in the backseat. He opened the back door and reached inside. "What are you doing?"

"Stay there. Keep watching for traffic."

Marc was grateful she did as she was told. He took the messenger bag first and opened its flap. Textbooks. A notepad. Nothing he could use. Marc went for the backpack next, and found a red-and-white scarf balled up beside more textbooks and a makeup bag. Brandi didn't say anything when he took the scarf and used it to stop MJ's bleeding.

MJ didn't say anything, either.

"He's still breathing, but he's not responding." Marc started to pull him up. "I need you to help me put him in the car." He pointed to the passenger side's back door. "You get in and help pull him across the back." Marc cradled MJ's head as he lifted him from the ground. The back of the college kid's head felt warm and wet, but Marc waited until he and Brandi had him curled up in the back of Honda to ask about it. "Why is the back of his head bloody?" He closed the car door.

Brandi closed the door on her side. "He hit his head when the animal bit him. That's why he's knocked out, right?"

"Probably." Marc looked back to the trees on the opposite side of the road. A slight breeze pushed the branches back and forth, and he still couldn't see any better in the dark. He turned back to Brandi. "Start the car and turn on the heater. Keep him warm."

"He's going to be okay, right?"

"How far away are we from the nearest town?"

"A few hours."

"You probably want to get him to a hospital and make sure he didn't get anything from . . . what bit him?"

"I don't know. A dog. A wolf. Something like that."

"Get in my car."

"What? Why?"

Marc wasn't listening to Brandi anymore; he was listening to the night, the trees, the wind. And the faint howl he heard somewhere in those woods. He already knew what time of the month it was, but he glanced up at the sky anyway.

It would be two days before the moon was full, but it was close enough that he suddenly felt naked without his Beretta. Or his silver bullets.

Brandi hadn't moved from her Honda by the time he reached his own car's driver door.

"Move!"

"But I can't leave MJ. You said to take him to a hospital."

Marc stomped back toward her. "Later. We need to talk. In my car." He grabbed her shoulders. "Got it?"

He guided her back to his rental and helped her into the passenger seat. When he got to his side of the car and sat down himself, Brandi was shaking. "What's happening? Why are we doing this?"

She flinched when Marc reached across the seat, and tried to push away when he opened the glove box. He made sure Brandi saw he was retrieving his Beretta. He needed her to do as she was told for now, and if that meant frightening her a little, that was better than the potential alternative. "Tell me what happened."

"What?"

"What did you two hit with your car?"

"Why does it matter? What are you going to do to me?"

"It matters a lot." Marc cocked his head. He thought he might have heard another howl, and this time it was closer. "And I'm going to keep you alive."

"What?"

"Shut up." Marc rolled down his window. That was definitely a howl.

He looked at his Beretta, and shook his head since its rounds were standard 9mm variety. The Pocatello job was not a lycanthrope elimination, so he wasn't prepared for this. If this was even a werewolf problem. Marc rolled his window up most of the way and stared at Brandi. He'd scared her, and thick tears lined her lower eyelids, but she hadn't started to full on cry yet. Hopefully he could keep it that way. "I'm sorry, Brandi, but this is important. I need to know what you hit with your car."

She blinked, but she kept her tears under control. "I told you. It was a dog or coyote or something."

"You said it was a wolf."

"Yeah. Maybe. I don't know. I'm not from around here. Why - "

Marc held his free hand up to Brandi's face, silencing her. He heard it again, and this time, it wasn't alone. There were at least two of them outside and getting closer. He looked back at Brandi. She still wasn't crying. That was good, but he didn't want to push it. "I need to get something out of the trunk. And I need you to stay here. You got that?"

When Brandi didn't answer fast enough, Marc hardened his stare. She finally nodded.

Marc opened his car door and slid into the night. It felt cooler outside, but Marc didn't know if the temperature had actually dropped or if he was letting those approaching howls get to him. He corrected himself - the howls themselves shouldn't bother him. That he was so unprepared was what shook him. The job in Pocatello - the guy on his voicemail described what Marc figured was a poltergeist or doppelgänger problem - didn't sound like it would call for silver bullets, so Marc didn't have any loaded. His old bosses would have been happy as he wasn't wasting resources by bringing everything out in the field. He reminded himself that one of the reasons he quit the Bureau was because the policies and the paperwork and the bureaucracy and all those reports got in the way of his doing his job. And if there were more than a couple werewolves out there, he might not ever get to that job in Pocatello.

He popped the trunk and part of him hoped that he'd packed a case of silver bullets and just forgot. All of him hoped he wouldn't need them since he knew otherwise. What he did have was his go bag, a suitcase, and whatever the rental car agency stowed in the trunk. He didn't think the spare tire would help.

But the silver dagger in his luggage might.

Two distinct howls rippled through the night, each one coming from either side of the road.

Marc found his dagger in his suitcase, took it and some extra magazines for his Beretta and his back-up weapon - a Derringer he normally wore in an ankle holster. He hated driving while wearing it. He shot a reproachful glance at the gibbous moon and swore that it was too close to being a full moon for his liking.

"Hey! Are you going to check on MJ?"

Marc slammed the trunk down. Brandi's head leaned out of her open window. Marc scowled at her until she pulled back inside the car and rolled up the window. She asked a good question, though. He knew he should check on him. Marc knew there was enough blood on the road to attract unwanted wildlife attention, were- or otherwise.

Brandi started to roll her window down again as Marc walked by the passenger side of the rental. He made sure she saw him slide Derringer into his leather jacket pocket. She rolled her window back up again.

MJ lay in a fetal position in the back of the Honda. He was still breathing, and if not for his hitting his head, he should probably be awake. He hadn't bled enough to be unconscious. Marc didn't open the car door. If there were werewolves, the Honda's doors wouldn't stop them, but if it were just an animal -

Marc's ears tensed when a nearing howl ripped into a threatening growl. He spun to face the dark trees on his side of the road. Two pin pricks of angry light glowed somewhere deep in the trees. He held the silver dagger at the ready, letting its length run alongside his forearm.

Marc watched those two points of lights. They blinked once, but didn't move. Marc watched them closely, letting his own eyes lock with the werewolf's in the trees.

So much so that he was surprised when the other werewolf landed on the roof of his rental.

Marc jerked around. His eyes stared into the eyes of this other werewolf. Yellow-eyed animal rage stared back at him. Under the light of the pale moon, its fur might have been dark gray, but the Honda's emergency lights flashed vibrating white across its body. Marc tried to look past it to see if any other werewolves might emerge from the other side of the road, but he lost sight of everything for a moment. The other werewolf hit him from behind. He heard his leather jacket tear under its claws, but being slammed against the rental car distracted him enough to keep him from noticing if he was bleeding. Brandi screamed.

Marc fumbled for the car door handle, but the door wouldn't open.

Under normal circumstances, Marc would have just rolled his eyes. But he hadn't had the luxury of living under normal circumstances in a long time. The werewolf on the roof reminded him of that when it snapped at Marc with its wicked jaws. Marc let his legs uncoil and he slid down the side of his car. He flexed his fists and was pleasantly surprised that he still held his silver dagger. He couldn't get at the werewolf above him from this angle, but if the other one was still behind him?

He swung his arm back, blindly stabbing, and stopping when he heard something yelp. The werewolf on the rental's roof leaped over him to join its hunting companion.

Marc didn't bother to turn around. He yelled at Brandi instead. "Open the door!"

When Brandi hesitated, he scrambled around the car to get to the driver's side. He beat her to that door and opened it before she locked him out. Brandi shrank back from him, seeming to forget the werewolves on her side of the road. Marc didn't remind her. Instead, he reached behind to check his back. It seemed like his jacket took most of the damage. He'd replace it later.

If he ever made it to Idaho.

Brandi made sounds as if she was about to start screaming again. Marc put his free hand up. Her lips quivered, but she didn't open her mouth. But she was still in the way. Marc tried to look around her, but she squirmed too much. Then she looked through the windshield, and started screaming again. He saw why when he looked out the windshield himself.

Standing between his car and Brandi's Honda, illuminated by headlights and the gibbous moon, were the two werewolves. Marc made a mental note to remind himself to never be caught this close to a full moon without silver bullets again.

One of the werewolves expanded its muscled chest, looked to the sky, and howled. The other locked eyes with Marc and curled its lower lips back to expose its sharp canine teeth.

Marc didn't have time to determine which of the werewolves was the one he stabbed earlier. He reached for the car keys, started the engine and slammed his foot down on the accelerator. The car's transmission shuddered when he popped the gear shift. He kept the wheel steady but spared a quick glance at Brandi. "Brace yourself!"

Brandi put her arms in front of her and pressed her hands on the dashboard. Marc tensed his arms and leaned forward. He took a quick breath, clenched his teeth and hoped he could keep the car straight when he hit the werewolves.

He did.

The rental car slammed into the lower bodies of the two monsters. Something cracked underneath the car's hood, but Marc kept his foot on the gas. The werewolves bent over the front of the car, clawing at its sides, trying to find something to hang on to as Marc sped toward the Honda in front of them. Howls turned to quick, pained yelps when he hit Brandi's car.

He pushed his body back into the car seat to keep from crushing his chest against the steering wheel. Marc kept his foot on the pedal, and once the ringing in his ears stopped, he heard a satisfactory mix of spinning car tires and whimpering werewolves. The car pushed forward, pinning the two monsters between the vehicles. The Honda's emergency lights still throbbed, flashing awkward beams of light around the two angry werewolves. Marc kept his foot on the gas but turned to Brandi. It didn't take too long for his cold glare to stop her yelling. "I need you to take over."

Brandi sniffled. "What?"

The car shifted back. Marc looked up and saw that one of the werewolves was now standing and trying to work a hand-claw-paw-whatever underneath the car.

Marc didn't let up. The wheels squealed on the asphalt. "I have to get out of the car. But I need you to take over. Keep the gas on." He looked at Brandi again, and tried to keep any panic out of his voice and face. "Can you do that?"

Brandi started to shake her head, but jumped when the car jerked to the side.

"Brandi. Look at me. I'm going to go check on MJ."

Brandi responded with a tiny nod.

"Okay. Good. Hop over to the driver's seat as fast as you can when I get out."

He didn't wait for a response. Marc made sure he had his silver dagger ready and opened the car door.

He heard the tires stop crying against the road as he stood, but only long enough to hear Brandi scramble into the driver's seat and stomp on the accelerator. He closed the car door and stepped out of reach of the werewolves.

The one closest to him stopped trying to move the car and stared at him. Its yellow eyes frowned into angry slits and a loud, meaty growl spilled from its snout. Beside it, the other werewolf continued to paw at the car, but it didn't have the leverage to move it more than a few inches in any direction.

Marc looked at his silver dagger, and mentally measured its length. He took a step back, and considered his only options.

He could only think of one.

The attentive werewolf twisted and tried to watch Marc as he backed up and away from the werewolves. Marc hoped it would keep trying to watch him even as he moved to the front of Brandi's car, even if that meant it would see him coming. He spared a quick look in the back seat of Brandi's Honda. MJ lay still where they left him. Over the burning wheels, Marc could hear the pained howls of the creatures still trying to free themselves. He mentally labeled them Target One and Target Two. Target One twisted its head back and forth, turning as much as it could to keep Marc in its sight. Marc knew it would see him coming. He still didn't like his option.

But if the werewolves got free, he would like his chances even less. Marc climbed onto the Honda's hood. The car trembled as the werewolves continued to work to free themselves, but Marc kept his balance.

He didn't have any cover. The werewolf knew he was coming. He didn't know if the monster knew he was armed with a silver dagger, but he didn't have any choice.

The car shifted a few inches. Marc's hands flew from his sides as he tried to keep upright. One of the werewolves still focused on trying to free itself from between the cars. The other snapped its body and head back and forth, watching Marc.

Marc made it to the windshield of the Honda and pushed himself to the roof. If the werewolf was facing the other way, he knew it might be able to reach him by now. Even turned and twisted the way it was, the beast might still connect with a backhanded swing.

A cool breeze drifted through the back of his ruined jacket. Marc crouched, and pulled his dagger hand back. The werewolf alternated between trying to reach over its shoulder and swinging its arms back, but Marc managed to stay out of reach. He steadied himself and tightened his grip on the silver dagger.

Past the writhing werewolves, through the windshield of his rental car, he saw Brandi's white knuckles shaking on the steering wheel as she stared back at him. Marc tried to encourage her with a quick nod.

And then he lunged at Target One's back.

Marc hated fighting lycanthropes hand-to-hand. The danger of being physically overpowered aside, he just didn't like to get too close to them. They smelled. Their fur felt like steel wool cut at the wrong angle. And their skin was usually too thick to land anything but a glancing blow. But coming at a werewolf from behind gave Marc a slight advantage, and he buried the blade of his dagger into the werewolf's back just below its left shoulder. He tried to hang onto the dagger, to keep pushing the silver blade, but the werewolf violently shuddered and Marc couldn't keep his grip. The cars shifted again, and this time he lost his balance and fell back. Hard.

Marc didn't think about bruising his tail bone just then. He didn't think about the body of the college kid curled up in the backseat of the Honda he was bouncing across - the body he thought he saw move as he scrambled up the car's back window. He didn't think about his own rental, and he didn't think about the job in Pocatello.

He did think about how much he would have charged for a job like this, but shook that thought from his mind as he slid on his back to the roof of the car.

He reached out with both hands to find the upper edge of the car's back windows on either side of Honda. Both werewolves howled; both werewolves shook the cars as they tried to twist their way free. Marc squared himself, pulled back his right foot and didn't have to wait long for the injured werewolf to present his stuck back right where Marc wanted it.

He kicked. His boot heel connected with the base of the dagger's handle.

The werewolf shrieked. Marc pushed himself further away from them and slid headfirst and backward down the windshield of the Honda. He caught a glimpse of MJ sitting up in the backseat, but decided to deal with that later. He just hoped the kid wouldn't do anything stupid.

By the time Marc got the pavement under his feet again, MJ was getting out of the car. Stupid. Marc drew his Beretta and pointed it at

MJ. "Get back in the car!"

MJ wasn't paying any attention to Marc. He took a tentative step toward the werewolf now laying still, draped over Marc's rental. Marc didn't like being ignored. He aimed and pulled the trigger.

MJ jumped back, but not because Marc was aiming at him. Marc was shooting at the other werewolf. He didn't expect to do any lasting damage, but didn't want to fire blindly. On the other hand, now both MJ and the werewolf were both staring at him. Marc addressed MJ first. "In the car."

MJ did as he was told. Marc turned his attention to the remaining car-sandwiched werewolf. It stared back at him, its clouded eyes narrowing as it peeled back its lips. There was no way Marc was getting his silver dagger back. He looked up at the moon and cursed it, but then he had an idea.

He looked back at the werewolf and stepped closer to it. He kept the still form of its companion between him and it. He didn't want to give it an opportunity to snag him if it reached for him. The beast kept its gaze on him as he passed the screeching tires of his rental, and when he reached the driver's door, he knocked on the window with his free hand. "Turn it off."

He looked down at Brandi. She looked confused.

"Stop the car."

She finally nodded and shifted in the driver's seat. The tires slowed, and the car's engine rumbled to a stop.

Marc returned his attention to the werewolf. He held his Beretta in front of him, keeping it pointed at the creature. Marc hoped it didn't hear him take a deep, reassuring breath before he spoke. "You know this gun can't really hurt you." He slid it into his pocket and retrieved his Derringer. "But this one can."

The werewolf didn't seem to understand at first. Marc made sure it saw the handgun. "Hey! I'm talking to you!" He pointed the Derringer at the moon. "That thing's not full. You can still hear me, right?" He took aim at the werewolf. If he fired, he'd hit it in the skull, maybe even get through that thick bone and into the monster's brain, but he knew it wouldn't stop the werewolf for long without silver bullets. He continued his bluff. "So here's how this is going to work. We'll let you go, and you can limp home. We'll be on our way, and you'll be on yours." Marc ventured a step forward. "Do you understand?"

Marc felt that breeze through the back of his ruined jacket again. He thought he saw Brandi and MJ moving in their respective cars, but he kept his focus on the werewolf. "You can at least nod if you understand me."

Marc thought if he was fast enough, he might get close enough to rip the silver dagger from the dead werewolf's back before the other lycanthrope could react. But he didn't like the idea of matching his speed against that of a monster like this, even if the monster was already pinned between two cars. This might have even been the one he stabbed earlier.

He shook his head. He still didn't like his odds.

When the werewolf nodded back at him, Marc tried to suppress a sigh of relief. "Good. Now let's be clear about something. We're going to let you go, and then you can limp away." Marc punctuated his words with a thrust of his Derringer. "I'll move your buddy there to the side of the road, and you can come back for him long after we've driven off. Or not. I don't really care."

Marc knew that by the time the morning sun scared the near-full moon off, the dead werewolf's body would melt back into its human form. He'd rather not have the authorities investigating a random dead body on the side of the road halfway to Idaho, and hoped its werewolf family would claim the body. "Do we understand each other?"

The werewolf huffed and nodded again.

"Good." Marc kept his gun pointed at the pinned werewolf, but looked over to Brandi. He didn't have to catch her attention. Her focus was more on him than the monster.

"Back up. Slowly." He cringed at the sound of his rental car's grinding transmission. That would cost him. He tried not to get lost in thoughts of charging the extra rental car's fees to his client in Pocatello and returned his attention to the live werewolf.

It relaxed and fell to all fours as it was finally freed from the cars. The dead werewolf flopped on the ground next to it. Marc kept his Derringer trained on the live monster, but took a step back. He gestured toward the trees with the gun.

"Go on, boy. Get."

The werewolf sniffed at its dead companion before slowly turning and limping into the darkness. Marc's sigh caught in his throat when he heard something moving behind him. He spun around, and saw a large man standing on the other side of the road. He wore loose-fitting running pants and a dark t-shirt that fit him just as well.

Marc raised his gun in the man's direction. "Don't tell me. You're a werewolf, too."

The man tilted his head back and loosed a howl into the night sky. Marc inched back until he could reach down and pull the silver dagger from the werewolf corpse. The man crossed the street, and only hesitated when Marc brought the silver blade in front of him.

"Why don't you run off now, too?" Marc knew if this so-called man transformed and charged, he couldn't be fast enough. The silver dagger would help, but not enough.

MJ opened the car door. In the time it took Marc to glare at him and hope that it was enough to keep MJ from getting out of the Honda, the unchanged werewolf leaned forward and sniffed at the Derringer. Marc kept his dagger ready.

The man cocked his head and grinned at Marc. "Doesn't smell like silver."

Before Marc could bring his dagger up, the man stepped back. Marc felt his eyes lock onto his own. This werewolf might not have allowed himself to transform under the moonlight, but Marc knew he'd still be trouble if he had to fight him now.

MJ slid from the car and closed the door behind him. "What's going on?"

Marc was about to answer MJ, to tell him to get back in the car, to tell him that he was safer where he was, but then he heard Brandi open her car door. The werewolf-in-man-form might have chuckled.

Marc lowered the gun. "All right. Look. We don't want any trouble. Why don't you just move on and leave us alone. We can all have a good rest of our night."

Marc wasn't even convincing himself. But the werewolf man did seem to consider Marc's words. MJ stayed by the Honda, even when Brandi closed her car door behind her. Marc tried to keep them in his peripheral vision as he watched the man's eyes. He almost broke eye contact when the man shrugged.

"You can go."

Marc wasn't going to argue. He didn't lower his guard, though. "Brandi. Go around the other side of the cars. I'll be there in a second to talk with you and MJ." Brandi did as she was told.

"The boy stays. You killed one of my pack. I want a replacement."

Marc knew it wouldn't do much damage, but he raised the

Derringer again. "One of your pack?" The man howled again. Marc took that as confirmation. He was facing off against a pack leader. An alpha. A lycanthropic pain in his ass that wasn't happily going to back down against a human with a silver dagger and a handful of bold words. Marc was going to try anyway. "Go find someone else. We're done here." He hated the idea of turning any werewolves loose to eventually kill or, worse, turn someone else, but he didn't see an alternative here.

The alpha apparently had one in mind. "Let me talk to the boy."

"What?"

"You said his name was MJ?"

Marc looked at the college students. They stared back at him. He shook his head at neither of them. Marc took a sideways step toward his rental car. "You're free to talk to him. That's it."

The alpha grinned, and made sure Marc could see his canine teeth before nodding and turning toward MJ. Marc didn't wait. He snapped his arm around, and leveled his Derringer at the alpha's legs. The gun jerked in his hand when he pulled trigger, but his aim was true. One of the alpha's legs buckled, dropping him to his knees. His scream turned to a quick growl as he pivoted on the asphalt. Marc dropped the Derringer and ran at the alpha, raising his dagger in his right hand and hoping for the best. The werewolf started transforming by the time Marc wrapped his left arm around its neck. Fur sprouted beneath Marc's grip. He held on, and stomped on the back of the werewolf's injured leg, keeping it grounded. He felt the bones of the werewolf's back and shoulders shift and grind as they changed their shape. Marc heard something tear, but didn't bother to see what it was. The monster bucked and tried to shake him free, but Marc kept his arm snaked around its neck.

Marc knew the bullet wouldn't slow the werewolf down for long. When the werewolf finally got to its feet, the non-silver-bullet wound was already starting to heal. But Marc held on, and raised the silver dagger in front of them and angled it at the werewolf's chest. The alpha turned and backed hard into the car. Marc's back threatened to bend a very wrong way against the Honda's roof. He clenched his teeth to keep them from rattling free when the werewolf took a step forward and then slammed back again. His grip on the dagger loosened, and he jerked down to keep it in his hand.

The werewolf straightened and spun. Marc felt his arm starting to slip. He saw MJ and Brandi brush past his vision twice before the monster bent over. The dagger threatened to slip from his hand. He curled his fingers in the werewolf's fur, but couldn't hold on any longer. Marc fell from the spinning monster, and rolled across the highway. What was left of his jacket protected his upper body as well as it could, but he knew he'd still have plenty of scratches and bruises to greet him tomorrow morning.

If he survived tonight.

When he came to a stop, he was face down with his head angled away from the cars. He couldn't see the college kids from his position, but he heard the werewolf. It growled and huffed as it stomp-pawed its way to Marc's body.

Marc tensed, and waited. He heard the heavy breathing, the sniffing, the angry panting of the werewolf on his back. Lukewarm drool fell on Marc's neck. He felt the monster's muzzle push against him. Marc willed himself not to react. He felt the werewolf press against his right shoulder. It shoved Marc, and then started to lift him. Marc let the monster try to flip him. After the second nudge, Marc allowed himself to turn over. As he turned onto his back, he brought his right hand up as fast as he could. And the silver dagger found its home in the werewolf's chest.

The monster shrieked and jumped back. Marc scooted away so he could stand.

The werewolf's body shuddered as a pained howl bubbled from its throat. It flipped itself onto its back, and pawed at the offending dagger.

Marc couldn't have that, especially since it was slower reverting to its human form. Before it had control of its thumbs again, Marc moved to front of the werewolf and, kneeling, held the dagger down. He leaned his weight into it, and looked into the monster's eyes as they shrunk into something more human-sized. He held the dagger in place long after the werewolf had completely returned to human form, and even longer after it stopped breathing.

The dagger came out easy after that.

Marc surveyed the highway as he stood. Blood. Torn pants. His Derringer. Dead werewolves. Two cars that had seen better days, and two college kids in the same condition. Almost. There was the matter of MJ.

He should probably just take care of him now. It would save a lot of time and trouble. And the two kids were probably both in shock. It wouldn't be too difficult.

Marc looked at his bloody silver dagger, then looked at MJ.

MJ's body shook. "Oh, god."

Brandi looked at him, then looked at Marc.

Marc recognized the look on her face. He'd seen it many times before with clients. She wanted to disbelieve. She wanted to pretend she could somehow will herself to unlearn what she'd just learned. But she couldn't. Not now. Not after what she just lived through.

MJ just looked scared.

Marc knew what he probably should do.

But that's not what he did. "MJ. Get in your car." Marc was glad he didn't have to argue with him.

"Brandi. We need to talk."

"About what?"

Marc shook his head, and picked up his Derringer. After pocketing it, he moved to the dead alpha and grabbed its legs. As he pulled it off to the side of the word, he looked up at Brandi. "Just get in my car. Passenger side."

After dragging the dead werewolf into the tree line, Marc went back to the highway. He couldn't clean up all the blood. With any luck, it would rain soon and wash some of it away.

He made sure nothing of his was left behind before getting back into his rental car to talk with Brandi. "What do you think just happened out there?"

Brandi stared ahead. "I have no idea."

"I think you've got at least half of one. Reach in the glove box. There should be something to write with in there."

Brandi found a pen. "What are you going to do with us?"

"There something to write on in there?" She pulled out a brochure from the rental agency.

"Write this down." Marc gave her his phone number.

"What's this for?"

"What happened out here tonight will probably happen again. You said MJ was bit, right?"

Brandi nodded.

"So sometime next month, he's going to change."

"Change?"

"Like you saw earlier."

"And what am I supposed to do with this phone number?"

"If he needs to be put down, you call me." Marc waited for Brandi to ask another question. When she didn't, he nodded at her. "You can go now."

Brandi got out of the car, and Marc drove off.

ARE YOU MY MUMMY?

"I don't do partners." Marc Temple eyed the film student behind the video camera. "And I don't do media."

Nick Franklin glanced over his shoulder at Josh, the sideburned third-year film student from Bozeman. "He's not recording. You'd see that red blinking light." He looked back at Marc and brought his cup of coffee to his lips. He paused and smiled. "And the lens cap would be off."

Marc pushed his chair away from the dinette table. "Dammit, Nick. I'm done. You don't have a job here for me. I have one lined up in Washington, and I already missed my train thanks to you."

Nick finished his coffee and despite his missing his first two fingers of his right hand, delicately set it down on the table top. "I already told you. I'd pay you if I could."

"But it's not in your budget."

"It's not good business."

Marc shook his head. "How is it good business to not get paid for my services?"

"No. It's not good business for me." With his full-fingered left hand, Nick made a shooing motion at Josh. Josh nodded silently and shuffled toward the door. Nick didn't wait for Josh to leave before continuing. "I'm putting this on YouTube and I have a budget to keep. I'm already paying for your room. If I pay you your normal rate, I'd be in the red."

Marc waited until the door closed and leaned closer to Nick. "You're already in the red. Who are you trying to kid? YouTube? Really?" He pushed away again. "There were rumors about you before you left the Bureau, and you didn't exactly keep a low profile after your early retirement." He stood and lifted his jacket from the back of the chair. "Unlike you, I am keeping a low profile and I can't do that if I star in some video produced by some ex-FBI-agent-slash-bankrupt author."

"I'm not bankrupt."

"And while I appreciate that you kept my name out of your books, I can't let you put me on tape." Marc moved toward the tripod and stepped behind the camera. "You sure this isn't on?"

Nick turned in his chair. "It's not tape. It's digital. And I wouldn't ask you to do this if I wasn't desperate. I think it would be good for you, too. More exposure means more clients, right?"

Marc decided the camera was turned off. "I get phone calls and I don't have to advertise."

"But you can do so much more, Marc. You and I both know it."

Marc looked at the ceiling and sighed. "I don't need to do more. I'm doing just fine financially."

"I'm not talking about money. I'm talking about helping people."

"You're talking about helping you out of a mess."

"Call it what you want." Nick strummed the three fingers of his right hand on the table. "I need you, Marc. I can't call anyone else. I'm on the black list."

"You put yourself there when you didn't get tested after Oklahoma City."

Nick stopped strumming. "There was nothing wrong with me after that."

"A werewolf ate half your hand, Nick."

"He only got two fingers."

"And you didn't turn."

"I know. That's why I didn't get tested. I didn't need to."

Marc slowly walked back to the little, round table. "That's exactly why you should have been tested. To find out why." He sat back down. "That was selfish."

Nick shrugged. "They would have locked me in a silver cage for who knows how many full moons until someone higher up decided I was still normal."

"It wasn't normal."

"Your paranoia about me is making my point. The Bureau wouldn't have trusted me anymore."

"No one trusts you now."

"But at least I get to call my own shots."

"As what? An independent contractor?"

"Isn't that what you do?"

Marc shook his head and started to respond, but stopped himself. Even though they were never officially partners, Marc and Nick worked plenty of jobs together, and too many fast-food-and-bad-coffee-fueled stakeouts ended with Nick talking him in circles about Bureau policy. He didn't miss those conversations, and wasn't going to let Nick bait him like he used to. Instead, he sat down and used the fastest way he could think of to wrap this up.

"What do you want me to do?"

Nick clapped his hands and rubbed his palms together. "Excellent!"

"Not really."

"Don't be so negative, Marc. This is a win-win for both of us."

"If it ends with you losing my phone number, you're absolutely right. Just tell me about the case."

Nick gestured at the camera. "The film student you kicked out of the room? A few of his classmates disappeared, and we need you to find them."

"And this involves people with our background how?"

"They went Blair Witch-ing in a small town called Nickel."

Marc shifted in his chair. "Blair Witch as in they were making a movie or they were investigating a witch?"

"I'm still convinced that movie was real and the so-called actors that did the talk shows were doppelgängers."

"So we're dealing with doppelgängers?"

Nick shook his head. "No. The film students were making a documentary about some small haunted church in Nickel, found something, then disappeared."

"How did you get involved?"

"Josh contacted me through a comment I left on his YouTube page."

Marc rolled his eyes. "You're that hard up for work? You're trolling the internet?"

"No. I'm not, as you say, hard up. And I'm not, as you said earlier, bankrupt. I'm doing just fine, thank you very much."

"If that's the case, you can pay me."

Nick pulled back in his seat. "Well, I'm not doing that fine. Besides, most of my money is tied up in a new project. It doesn't matter. We're getting off track."

"Fine. You have a laptop? Can I see the video?"

"I had it pulled down."

"You have a contact at YouTube?"

"I just filed enough copyright infringement forms and the video got yanked. You know, like what happened to Lady Gaga, who I also think is a doppelgänger."

"Stop. You're making me want to leave again."

"Okay, okay. Anyway, I don't have the video, but Josh saved it to a hard drive or flash drive or something. I've seen it, and it made me think of you."

"Should I be flattered?"

"Only if you like haunted churches."

Marc felt his eyes roll. "You thought you saw a ghost, and then you thought of me? What do you take me for, Nick? Have you ever seen a ghost?"

Nick looked away. "Well . . . no."

"Not even on your film student's video?"

"No."

If he left right now, Marc thought he might be able to make a later train tonight and still make it to Washington tomorrow.

"Look, I know what the Bureau's stance is on ghosts."

"They're not real."

Nick shook his head. "And they said I shouldn't have survived a werewolf attack, and yet here I am."

Marc started to respond, but Nick held up his disfigured hand.

"I'm not saying there are ghosts in Nickel. These film school kids probably didn't either, but they thought it would make a good class project. They broke into the town's old church, tried to spend the night, and ended up disappearing. You can watch the video while Josh drives you there."

"Are you being mysterious on purpose? What's on the video?"

Nick shook his head. "I don't want to tell you what I think it is. It's probably not a ghost."

"Probably?"

"Okay. It's not a ghost. It's solid. But you should watch the video for yourself. It's not that long, so you can review it a few times before you get to Nickel."

His scowling was giving him a headache, but Marc couldn't stop. "You're not coming?"

"No." Nick stood and started for the door. "I have other business to attend to."

"Like what?"

"It doesn't matter. I mean, it does, but you wouldn't be interested."

"You're probably right."

"I'll be here at the motel when you get back. I'll have Josh load up the car and you can leave tomorrow morning."

"Wait a minute." Marc stood and followed Nick to the door. "How much does Josh know? About what we do, who we are, that sort of thing?"

Nick nodded. "I told him enough to keep him from going to the police. And I ran a check on him."

"How?"

Nick refused to answer and grinned. "Josh is a good kid, and if he gets through this okay, I'd like to involve him in my future plans." Nick placed his three-fingered hand on Marc's shoulder. "So bring him back in one piece, okay?"

"I already told you." Marc moved enough to let Nick's hand fall off of him. "I don't do partners."

The film student scored a couple of bonus points with Marc the next morning. Josh didn't make him wait in the parking lot, and he had a cup of coffee ready for him. They were on the road for about an hour before Josh started asking questions.

"Mr. Franklin said you would be armed, but you don't have any other equipment?"

Marc looked up from Josh's laptop and paused the video he was watching. "What did you expect?"

Josh didn't look away from the road. It was a clear day and they hadn't passed any traffic, but he still seemed nervous. "I'm not sure. I just thought that . . . " His voice drifted off and he tightened his grip on the steering wheel.

"What did Nick tell you?"

Josh took a moment to respond. "He said he knew someone who could help me find my friends."

"That all?"

"Yes, sir." Josh started to turn his head toward Marc, but stopped and flexed his steering wheel grip again.

"But?"

Josh sighed. "I just expected more. You saw the video."

Marc closed the laptop. "I've watched it a few times now, and I'm still not sure what I'm looking at. Do you have any ideas?"

"No, sir."

"So until I know more, I'm not dragging a bunch of tools with me to some small town in the middle of Montana. If we need more equipment, we can get whatever we need and come back." He forgot that he already finished his coffee, checked the cold cup, and dropped it back in the cup holder. "Did Nick tell you how he knew me? What we did before?"

Josh nodded.

"Did he tell you how he lost his fingers?"

The film student forced a smile. "Yes, sir. But I didn't believe him."

"Are you calling my friend a liar?"

"Mr. Franklin told me you weren't friends."

Marc laughed. "If he told you he lost his fingers fighting a werewolf, he was telling the truth."

"I still don't think I believe it." Josh's back stiffened. "Not that I'm calling you a liar, sir."

"Believe us or not, that's what happened. And that's just the tip of it. We've both lost more than Nick's fingers doing what we did before in the Bureau."

"The FBI?"

Marc nodded.

"Like in *The X-Files*?"

Marc frowned. "First off, no. Not like in *The X-Files*. And second, they were chasing aliens. We were chasing things that are much worse."

"Like werewolves?"

"Yes."

"And what else?"

Marc shook his head. "Take your pick."

Josh took a turn at shaking his own head. "I guess the horror movies have to come from somewhere, right?"

"Go with that. Go with what you know." Marc turned his attention to the window and watched the dry Montana summer landscape dust by. "Some of the movies get it right anyway."

"You sound like Steve Martin in *Grand Canyon*."

"What?"

"He plays a producer and tells Kevin Kline that all of life's answers can be found in the movies."

Marc shrugged. "I suppose so." He watched Josh. "You're taking all of this in stride. You know this probably isn't going to end the way the movies end for your friends."

Josh blinked and stared at the road ahead. "I know. I saw the video."

The next several miles passed in silence. Marc opened the laptop and reviewed the video again.

"Why weren't you with them?"

"Sir?"

Marc looked up from the video. "Why didn't you go with your friends to Nickel?"

"I had to work."

"But you're part of this school project?"

Josh nodded. "I'm going to be the editor." He thought for a moment and corrected himself. "I was going to be the editor."

Marc looked at the silent image on the screen. "Why isn't there any sound?"

"I don't know. They checked out some audio equipment, so maybe we'll find it at the church."

Marc nodded.

"Do you think they're dead, sir?"

"What do you think?"

Josh was quiet for another mile. "I don't know."

"Do you think it's real? The video, I mean. Could it be staged?"

Josh shook his head. "We didn't bring in any actors."

"They could have found someone in Nickel."

"I don't think so, sir. Our class assignment was to produce a documentary. Mr. Franklin already asked me all these questions." He spared a glance at Marc. "No, I don't think they're pulling a prank. No, I really haven't heard from them by phone or email. No, I don't think any of this is funny." He looked back at the road. "I've watched that video more than either of you, and all I see is my friends screaming and being chased by something that breaks out of a wall. It's dark, so I ran it through some filters, and I still don't know what I'm looking at, but I think it's real, and I'm scared." He took a deep breath. "Sir."

"What were their names?" Marc caught himself. "What are their names?"

"Jennifer was directing. Kylie was running sound and Stephen checked out the camera."

"So this is all the school's equipment?"

Josh nodded. "Most of it."

A complication. The school would want an accounting of the cameras and film gadgets. Marc hoped Nick could make that go away.

But he couldn't make Josh go away. Why did he bring the film student in? Nick told him about their past, their time at the Bureau, the werewolf attack that eventually took Nick off the government's payroll. Marc thought to ask Josh how much Nick told him about his own background, but the turnoff to Nickel crawled over the horizon.

Marc asked another question instead. "Have you ever been here? To Nickel?"

Josh shook his head. "No, sir."

He appreciated it at first, but this "sir" business was starting to grate on him. It was starting to remind him of his time in the Bureau and since that ended badly . . . "You can call me Marc."

"Okay."

"So. Nickel?"

"Kylie found out about it on some website. She said it would be an easy shoot since it wasn't too far away. She made some phone calls, got Jennifer in touch with someone there, and we were ready to go."

"Who?"

"Sorry?"

"Who was your contact in Nickel?"

"Oh. Right. Some librarian or caretaker or something. And I already tried talking to him."

"And?"

"He told me not to bother him again." Josh hit the turn signal and leaned the minivan toward the exit to Nickel. "He said he didn't give anyone any permission to film anything in a historical building and that he kicked everyone out of the church when he found out what we were up to." Josh pointed out the windshield. "I bet that's the church."

The Historic First Church of Nickel had seen better days, and Marc had seen better churches. It sat off the main road at the end of a short, dirt drive, alone if not for the tired mobile home squatting next to it. They pulled up to the church, found it locked, found the mobile home was being used as an office, but it was also locked. A handwritten sign on the office door listed a phone number, limited office hours, and a note proclaiming that all unattended vehicles left at the church would be towed at the owner's expense.

The church was octagonal, with one of its bricked sides extending as an entry hall that ended with double columns marking the steps leading up to a set of double doors. The brick and architecture placed the building's construction in the '50s, but Josh found a plaque on the door explaining that the church was rebuilt around the original wooden structure that served as Nickel's first church in the 1800s.

What Marc found at the doors was more interesting to him. Someone had broken the lock.

"Here's how this is going to work." Marc faced Josh. "I'm going in. You're staying in the van."

Josh started to protest, but stopped when Marc slipped his Beretta from his shoulder holster.

Marc caught the film student's eyes and followed them to his gun. "Relax."

"I want to go with you."

"No. I told Nick, and I'm telling you. I don't do partners."

"But my friends -"

"I know. I'll scope out the church, see what I can find, and if I need your help, I'll let you know."

"What if somebody comes by?"

Marc waited a long moment before responding. During that time, no cars drove by. "They won't. But if they do, tell them you're shooting your documentary. Grab one of your cameras and pretend to film something."

Josh slowly nodded.

"And here." Marc reached down for his ankle and retrieved his Derringer. He handed it to Josh. "If anything other than me or your friends come out of the church, shoot it."

The film student studied the gun in Marc's hand.

Marc sighed. "Take it."

"I've never shot a gun before."

"It's not hard. Just point and pull the trigger. Like in the movies." He knew it wasn't like in the movies, but hopefully Josh wouldn't need to fire the gun and find that out for himself. Besides, it was a single-shot Derringer and probably wouldn't do Josh any good anyway, but he needed to give Josh a reason to stay outside.

Josh took the gun before heading to the van to grab a camera and tripod. Marc turned back to the church and walked up the steps to the doors. The knelt and studied the broken lock. Amateur work.

He stood up and joined Josh at the van. "I want to watch that video again." He slid into the passenger seat and opened the laptop while Josh set up his camera outside.

Marc expected Josh to be a problem. He expected the kind of person he used to encounter in the field when he was on the government's payroll. Questions. Disbelief. Getting in the way. He went freelance so he wouldn't have to waste his time either explaining the truth to people or making excuses to cover it up. When someone hired him now, they already suspected something supernatural at work. Josh was a surprise. Marc expected him to be trouble from the beginning, but he'd taken direction just fine. Even then, Marc would still be happier when this job was over.

Except it's not really a job. Nick wasn't paying him.

Marc shook his head and hoped Nick would keep his word about losing his phone number. He still didn't trust him. Not entirely. That werewolf bite should have left more than a disfigured hand. Marc was there when it happened, and applauded Nick's determination to shove that silver necklace down the monster's throat, but Nick really needed to get himself checked out when they got back to the Athens office. If nothing else, they might have found what it was about Nick's blood or DNA or whatever that made him resistant to lycanthropy, but Nick was selfish.

Marc sighed and started the video.

The lack of audio made it harder to ID whatever it was that attacked Josh's friends. Did it growl? Scream? Breathe heavy or tell a joke? Anything would help.

It was definitely solid. And strong. He slowed the video and watched as plaster and paint burst from a wall behind the student Josh ID'ed as Jennifer. She looked genuinely scared. This wasn't a prank. He trusted Nick's judgment on that from the beginning. He may not have trusted Nick as a person anymore, but he knew Nick wouldn't have called him if he didn't think what he was seeing on Josh's laptop was real.

Josh said Jennifer was around five-foot-six, which placed the hole in the wall around five feet off the floor. Only the attacker's hand came out, and when it grabbed Jennifer's hair, she yanked forward, revealing some of its wrist. The image shook as another student - Josh identified this one as Kylie - reached for Jennifer and tried to free her from . . .

Just what is it?

Marc didn't know how to make the image larger on the screen, so he held the laptop to his face and squinted at the pixels. He watched it again. Was whatever it was in the walls wearing a glove? It looked old, but Marc couldn't tell if what he was looking at were pieces of wall or pieces of Jennifer's attacker left in Jennifer's hair.

He set the laptop back down in his lap and let the video continue normally. He'd watched all this before, but would one more look show him anything? There was Jennifer after the attacker talking soundlessly into the camera. There was the camera jerking around as another crack appeared in the wall behind her. And there was Kylie rushing in to swing what Josh said was a boom pole at the arm reaching at them again.

Whatever it was retreated back into the wall, and the camera operator - Stephen - rushed forward with his camera. He aimed the lens right into the hole, and then there was a rush of movement. Marc tried not to blink and carefully watched the video just before the flash of static he'd gotten tired of seeing at the end of the video clip.

That was it. Two hands reached for the camera. The thing was no longer in the walls as it jerked after Stephen. Its body was covered in dust, maybe wrapped in something. Maybe a cloak or a jacket? The camera light was knocked away by a swipe of the thing's hand. Something dragged across the camera lens just before the end of the video. It looked like . . . a cloth? A loose wrapping of some sort?

Marc sighed. This wasn't going to end well.

He checked his jacket pocket and retrieved his lighter. He didn't smoke anymore, but he was still prepared. It struck a flame on his first attempt. Good. He closed and set down the laptop, chose one of the video cameras with a mounted light, and stepped out of the minivan. He faced the church. He didn't want to have to set it on fire.

He stepped back to the church, pausing to place a hand on Josh's shoulder. "I'm going in. You good?"

"Yes, sir." He shook his head. "I mean, Marc."

Marc used the camera to light the entrance hall. The beam washed over the dusty hardwood floors and along the wallpapered walls as he padded down the hallway. A calendar on the right marked the year as 1983. If not for the sneaker footprints in the dust, Marc would have believed no one had been in the church since then.

He pushed the light forward and listened. The church sounded empty, but he doubted he was alone. Marc wasn't going to be taken by surprise. He shifted the camera from his right hand to his left, holding it now by a bar on top, shooting the light from waist level. The Beretta came out in his right as he took a few tentative steps down the hall. He paused at the open doors on either side to peer further inside.

Both were offices, and both were dusty. Undisturbed. No damage. No film students. He pulled those doors shut and continued deeper into the church. A set of wooden doors marked the end of the hall and the entry into the sanctuary. Footprints led clearly back and forth from the closed doors. There were scuff marks in the floor where the doors had opened and closed against the hardwood floor.

The doors themselves marked the true age of the church. The wood was old and hand carved, and there was an inscription, but the letters didn't make sense. Too many 'E's and 'U's mixed with 'R's and phrases he didn't understand. Definitely not English. The doors were set deep in their frames, and when Marc moved the light over the door jamb, he noted the clear difference in age between the doorway's construction and the rest of the hall. The wood floor spoke of the building's age, but the doors held years over it.

He reached forward with his left hand, tilted the camera to the ceiling to free a finger, and looped it around the ornate metal door handle. Holding the gun at the ready, he pulled open the door.

And saw an empty sanctuary.

He slipped in and let the door close behind him. There were pews, some were knocked over or shoved aside. And there were cracks and holes in the walls.

Marc let the camera hang at his side and watched the floor as he moved along the room's exterior. Scuff marks, footprints, and scratches in the floor led him to the damage in the walls. These walls were wood, and he could see the years in the broken horizontal slats. Layers of paint and stain were exposed, and splinters of aged wood hung from the openings like dead weeds.

He slowly came to a stop and lifted the camera. The onboard light slid into the crack in the wall. Behind the wood, he could see torn insulation and brick. The crack ran nearly to the floor, and even though there didn't seem to be a lot of room to maneuver behind the wood, Marc considered stepping inside. He poked the camera into the crack and shone the light down either side. More insulation on the floor, some exposed electrical wires, scrape marks . . . and footprints? He'd have to duck. It looked like the brick cut in to make room for the stained-glass windows near the ceiling line, but he could probably stand inside. It didn't look like he'd be the first.

Marc lifted a foot to step into the crack, but stopped when he noticed something clinging to the ragged edge near the floor. He glanced around the church first, noted that the doors were still closed, then knelt to examine the discoloration on the floor. He probably didn't need to. He'd seen enough blood to know what he was looking at.

Something made a scratching sound behind him.

Marc zipped the camera around and splashed the light over an upended pew. There were other cracks in different places in the walls, with just as much dust and damage along their edges. The only undamaged wall was the one opposite the double doors he used to enter the sanctuary. There were cobwebs and dust, and a large golden cross mounted on that wall that could use polishing, but the wall itself was undamaged.

Marc tilted his head and strained his ears. More scratching. A thump. Something behind the walls.

And it was moving.

Marc stepped to the center of the room, trying to track the scratches. He used the camera light to highlight various openings in the walls, hoping he could catch some movement behind the old wood.

The sound stopped.

Marc sighed.

He looked around the room again. The disturbance of the dust on the floor, the damaged walls and out of place pews made it clear that someone was in the sanctuary recently, but was it the film students? Marc expected to see a video camera, a set of lights, or even that boom pole. How did the video get uploaded to YouTube? A smartphone?

Marc picked the largest hole in the wall and watched it as he set the camera down on the floor. On their drive to Nickel, Josh gave Marc his friend's cell phone numbers and they tried calling them along the way. No one answered then, but Marc thought he'd try calling them again now. He pulled his disposable cell from his jeans pocket and hit redial.

A tinny bit of music he couldn't identify played softly somewhere in the church.

He followed the sound, picking the hole he guessed to be closest, and took the camera to peek inside.

A bundle of smudged and bloody clothing, a chunk of blonde hair and too many broken bones for him to count were tucked neatly behind the wall. Lumpy sponges of old insulation helped to keep the collection nested along the angle of the narrow hallway. Marc held the camera back since he could see by the ringing iPhone's pale blue light. Patches of dirt or grime could have been blood on the floor. What looked like strewn stones could have been teeth.

And there was definitely something holding the phone. Shaped like a man, its head was down and away from Marc as it crouched over the pile of human debris. Thick, molded, and mouldy wrappings strapped around its back and shoulders. Ancient fabric dangled to the floor. Chunks of its covering had been eroded away, exposing dried tissue or even bone beneath. The back of its skull looked like a forgotten basketball underneath tattered strips. The light from the iPhone haloed its head when it brought it to its face. The sound of hard plastic scraping on bone told Marc this thing was rubbing the iPhone against its cheek or jaw. Was it trying to answer the phone? Or eat it?

The bandages, the strength to break through walls, the state of its body all told Marc he was dealing with a mummy. And he knew he had to take a shot. He moved his Beretta to his left hand, leaned further into the hole, and took slow aim. The thing at the end of the makeshift passageway still hadn't noticed him. He had to take a shot now, maybe draw it out, get some maneuvering room, get it out of the building, then deal with it properly.

From where he stood, he could see the old gold cross ahead of him on one side of the wall and the thing on the other. He nodded at the cross, focused on his Beretta, and pulled the trigger.

He hated shooting left-handed. He missed.

But it still got the thing's attention. It threw the iPhone away, lunged to its feet, and spun. Its chest heaved against worn wrappings, its neck twisted in weathered bandages. Its face, though . . . moist? In the moment before the iPhone hit the floor, its light reflected off wet, leathery lips.

Then it was dark between the walls.

Marc double-stepped back from the wall, switching the gun from his left to his right. The thing in the walls howled, and then growled, poking its head out from the crack. In the pale stained-glassed-sunlight, Marc got a better look at the creature. It was wrapped in old rags, and looked exactly as he expected it to when he thought about Josh's video. Except for its face.

It had eyes.

And they locked onto Marc's before the thing opened its crazily pliable lips and howled.

Marc shot two more times, and this time didn't miss. It didn't matter. This thing only seemed annoyed by the rounds Marc placed in its chest.

He took another step back, took another shot, and slid behind one of the pews. The thing took a tentative step forward, dipping its bandaged foot around a patch of blue sunlight on the floor.

Marc glanced back to the double doors. He could reach them in a few seconds. He looked back at the creature.

It moved around a sliver of stained-glassed yellow sunlight on the floor and let its jaw drop. Thick saliva dripped to the floor.

Saliva? That didn't make sense. And did it just lick its lips? It still had a tongue?

This wasn't a mummy.

This was a problem.

If Nick was paying him, he's have doubled his fee.

Another growl, another dance around a patch of colored sunlight on floor, and the thing crawled over the top of a pew.

Marc took another step away, his gun raised, his back to the double doors.

He expected a smell, something old and dusty, like an old book or a long-lost baseball mitt. But this thing smelled rotten, like old meat. It smelled undead, but not Egyptian.

The not-Egyptian thing squirmed over another pew and reached for Marc. He'd seen that hand before. It was the hand that reached out of the wall in the film students' video. Its nails were ragged, one of the fingers was missing, and . . . was that skin?

Marc slid out from behind his pew and backed into the double doors. At least this thing wasn't moving too fast.

It watched him as it crawled over the benches. It blinked its eyes.

It had eyelids. And they were leaking pus.

Marc was wrong about this from the beginning. It couldn't be a mummy. It had to be something else. But what?

The thing froze when Marc's back bumped into the double doors. Marc tightened his gun grip, aimed at the thing's head, and began pushing out of the sanctuary. It didn't move after him. It only stood there, blinking, watching, drooling.

Marc shrugged and pulled the trigger.

It screamed as the round burst its forehead just above its right eye. Sodden wrappings, bone, and flesh fell behind it, but the thing didn't fall.

It glared at Marc and ran.

Marc leaned the doors open and backpedaled out of the sanctuary. He kicked the doors closed and took several steps back, keeping his Beretta ready and taking aim at where the thing's head would appear in the doorway.

When the doors didn't open immediately, he counted down a minute before taking a step forward. There was nothing. No sound. No scratching. Nothing on the other side of those doors.

It would have been so much easier if it had followed him out.

He reached the doors and reached out with his left hand. Keeping his gun ready, he opened the door.

And was face-to-face with the thing.

It stared more at the door than at him. Marc considered taking another shot, but wanted to conserve ammo. He also wanted to conserve time, and didn't waste it. The cigarette lighter came out and he flicked it to life. If it wasn't going to chase him out of the church, he'd have to take care of it here and now. He hated to let a fire loose inside, but if a headshot didn't take it down, this might be the only way.

When he reached forward with the lighter, its attention snapped back to Marc. It hissed, and a sour scent that smelled like the first time the team let Nick cook for them skipped over Marc's face. He blinked when it hit his eyes, and in that moment, it grabbed Marc's wrist. The lighter slipped from his fingers. When it hit the floor, the tiny flame died.

Marc yanked his arm back. It held tight, and Marc winced when its fingernails slipped under the cuff of his sleeve and dug into his skin. He moved the gun to its head and fired. The thing didn't let go. Marc made a quick decision, and dropped his gun. The thing pulled him further into the doorway. With his free hand, Marc grabbed at the frame and pulled against it. He felt the skin of his wrist curling beneath the thing's fingernails. It screamed - it sounded like water ripping through tissue paper - and pulled harder at him.

Marc used a boot to brace himself and threw as much force as he could against it. It continued to pull and scream, but he finally was able to pull away. It moved with him as Marc drug his arm back.

And when his wrist passed through the threshold of doorway, the thing yelped and quickly released him.

Marc kept the door open as he retrieved his gun. His lighter was just inside the sanctuary, but it lay at the thing's feet. He couldn't reach it without it grabbing for him again.

Marc noted that the bullet holes in its skull seemed to be smaller than before. "Great."

It hissed back at him in response.

Marc closed the door in its face.

The heavy doors weren't what kept this thing at bay. It didn't seem to like the doors, but when he pulled it through the doorway itself, it yanked back. Something kept it inside the church, and it wasn't just that.

It might not have been a mummy, but it still behaved like some sort of undead. But what? It avoided the beams of sunlight in the church itself. But was it the sun itself, or something with the stained-glass windows?

It didn't make sense, and Marc was tired of Nickel.

He had another thought and pulled the doors open again. The thing stood there, as if waiting for him. Its chest shook as it huffed and puffed at Marc. It started to reach for him, but stopped at the doorway's threshold.

Marc tried not to notice that the bullet holes he put in its head were now gone. He also tried not to notice that he could now tell what color its eyes were (they were green). He tried to look past the tuft of brown curls sprouting from its scalp so he could sight the cross on the wall behind it.

Even though some pews were turned over, there was still a clear path down the center of the sanctuary. Marc guessed it was maybe forty feet from the doors to the steps leading up to back wall and the cross hanging on it. He ignored the wet pain leaking out of his wrist and took a few deep breaths while backing up from the thing in the doorway. The gun was useless at this point, so he holstered it.

The creature snorted.

Marc shook his head and charged.

He caught it in the chest and worked to wrap his hands around its body. He was able to trap one of its arms, but its other hand grabbed at the back of Marc's neck. It was heavier than it looked, and Marc struggled to keep them both from tumbling to the floor. He tried to keep his momentum up and forward, but the thing struggled against him. Marc felt its gritty fingernails snag in his hair and yank at his scalp, but he pushed on.

It screamed when they stumbled through a beam of red-and-gold sunlight, and it released its hold on Marc's hair. Marc kept pushing, kept moving forward, kept looking at the cross. The thing fought and tried to grab Marc's hair again, but he jerked his head away, maybe straining his neck. It changed tactics, and instead of grabbing at Marc, it reached for a pew to stop their procession through the church.

They both came to a sloppy halt when it finally found purchase on one of the benches. Marc shoved and buried his shoulder into its chest. He heard and felt something crunch inside its rib cage. A scream rushed out its throat. Its breath threatened to blind him. Marc shifted his weight and tried changing shoulders, but the creature pushed back now.

Marc's boots slipped on the floor. His wrist throbbed in sync with the blood thrumming through his eardrums. He gritted his teeth and fought to keep his grip, but he felt it slipping. The thing squirmed out of his grasp, and Marc leaned back as it raised its arms above him.

Then something ran into Marc from behind.

And it didn't stop.

Marc fell into the creature and fought to keep his footing. He saw an arm reach around him from behind and grab a handful of the thing's rotted cloth. Marc appreciated the assist, but he struggled to not get sandwiched. The creature still held onto the lip of a pew. Marc brought his fist down on its fingers and shoved forward.

Marc caught himself smiling when it yelped. He bent his knees and continued to push. The thing lost its grip and fell back.

Marc looked up at the cross. Still about twenty feet away.

Marc realized who was pushing behind him.

"What do you want me to do?" Josh leaned into Marc's back and tried to push the thing away.

"I don't do partners." Marc shot a quick look at the film student and grinned.

Then the thing fell back.

Marc reached for a pew to hold himself up, but Josh's weight pushed him down to the floor. The creature squirmed beneath him and made snapping sounds with its jaws. Marc kept away from its face and braced himself against its arms as it swung up at him.

Marc twisted to help Josh squirm off his back. "Get the cross."

"What?"

Marc tried to turn his head enough to look at the film student, but the thing caught some of his hair in its teeth. He whipped his head around and headbutted its forehead. Something crunched.

Marc blinked his eyes. "Go get the cross. I have an idea."

"The cross on the wall?"

"Yes!" Marc put his left hand down on the thing's chest, trying to hold it to the floor. Josh hopped over him and scampered to the front of the church. The thing hissed and spit while Marc tried to ignore the burning pain in his wrist.

Josh struggled. "It won't come off!"

Marc brought a foot up and then down on the thing's stomach. Something else crunched. It screamed. Marc glared at Josh. "I can't hold it down forever! Pull it off the wall!"

Josh put his back to him and grunted as he pulled at the gold cross. Marc focused on the thing on the floor beneath him. It squirmed and tried to get away. It pulled against a pew, but when its arm passed through a shaft of blue from one of the windows, it jerked its hand back and whined.

Marc was able to draw his gun. He knew the bullets wouldn't stop the thing, so he brought the butt of the gun down on its head. Another crunch. Marc continued, only pausing to look up when Josh stumbled back to him with the heavy gold cross in his arms.

Its arms were easily as wide as Josh's shoulders. The film student was stronger than he looked, and he only needed to hold the cross up a little longer.

The thing's eyes widened when it saw Josh heaving toward them. Now it tried to scuttle away, back toward the doors, and Marc had to reach for a pew himself to hold it in place. He flicked his eyes at Josh. "Drop it."

"Drop it?"

This was a bad time for Josh to stop following orders. "Yes! On . . . whatever this is! Drop it!"

Josh tilted the cross forward and let it fall with a splattering thud on the not-quite-mummy.

Marc reached out and motioned for Josh to move around the thing as he himself stepped back. He would have said something, but he knew he wouldn't be heard. The thing screamed and tried to writhe away. It reached out with its jagged fingers, but when it touched the golden cross, it snapped its hands back and stopped screaming long enough to whimper.

They watched the thing struggle and deflate as they backstepped down the center of the sanctuary. Its screams winnowed into cries and eventually, it stopped making any noise at all. Josh kept his eyes on it, but leaned close to Marc. "What is it?"

"I don't know." Marc looked back at what he dropped earlier in the doorway. "But get my lighter."

On their way out of Nickel, Marc called the number they found on the mobile home office outside the church. He was sure someone would see the fire and alert the fire department eventually, but the fire didn't need to spread any further than it had to. After he left a voicemail and hung up, Marc took a breath and told the film student what Marc hoped he already knew. "Your friends were dead before we got there."

Josh slowly nodded.

"And most of the church will survive the fire if the fire department gets there soon enough. The brick will be fine. Do you need pull over to throw up again?"

Josh said nothing and continued to drive.

Marc's wrist burned. He didn't notice before how much he was bleeding, but he'd have to clean it up later. He just wanted to get back to the motel and get out of Montana.

When they pulled into the parking lot, Marc stopped Josh from getting out of the car right away. "You did good back there."

"But my friends are dead."

"They are. But you're not."

Josh looked at Marc and started to say something, but stopped and turned his gaze to the parking lot.

Marc slipped out of his seatbelt.

"You're leaving?"

"This job is done."

"Except Nick didn't pay you."

Marc grinned. "Remind him of that for me, okay? Give me something to write on."

Josh reached around and pulled out a notebook. Marc took it and the pen Josh also offered.

Marc shook his head as he wrote in the notebook. "Here's my number. If you need it, use it. Just do me a favor."

"What?"

"Don't tell Nick you have it."

2-FOR-1 CHINESE SPECIAL

(Originally published in
Leather, Denim & Silver: Legends of the Monster Hunter,
Pill Hill Press, 2011)

When the vampire's fist struck, Marc Temple's world exploded in a burst of white light. His vision returned quickly, dimming to the muted downtown night colors, but burst again when the second fist struck his chin. His returning vision slowed when the back of his head bounced against the flaking brick behind him. He heard a crunch - either bone or tooth - as he clenched his jaw, refusing to spit blood. As he slid down the wall, he grabbed for his Beretta hidden under his black leather jacket, but one of the two opponents - he couldn't tell which at the moment - snatched it away before he could wrap his bruised fingers around it.

"No, no, no, Mr. Temple. No." The younger-looking of the two brothers examined the gun while the other squarely pressed his boot into Marc's stomach. "No more shooting. Not that it mattered." The vampire puffed his chest in Marc's direction. Marc saw the two gunshot wounds were already closing.

Marc tried to shift his body, maybe stand, but he was pinned by the slender vampire.

The younger-looking of the two - Marc was able to finally identify Zhao - licked the barrel of Marc's Beretta. The slight point of his tongue snapped between his teeth. "You've already put a few shots in Zhen, and it didn't do you any good. The holes you put in my brother will be gone tomorrow. As you will, Mr. Temple."

Zhen slid the Beretta into the back of his pants. "We've kept a low profile for many years, and we don't appreciate you disrupting things in our city. Do we, Zhao?"

Zhao responded by rotating his foot slightly, twisting his steel-toe against Marc's sternum.

Marc shot his eyes around the alley. He wasn't surprised that no other exit materialized when he chased these two into this dead end fifteen minutes ago. No one responded to the gunshots. This was a big city - some cop might wander by to check it out, but Marc knew he couldn't count on the local law enforcement for the kind of assistance he would need.

He felt the boot pressing harder against his stomach. Marc focused his attention on Zhao and reluctantly coughed a gob of blood at the vampire's foot. Marc watched the glob trickle across the scuffed boot leather.

"Is that all you have left?" Zhen taunted.

Zhao smiled and reached down to his boot. He trailed his thumb through the red spit, and when he shifted to bring the bloody appetizer to his mouth, Marc sprung.

Or, at least, he tried to. He managed to get to his feet, but by the time he was there, Zhen had changed positions with Zhao, who was now contentedly sucking on his thumb. Zhen seized Marc by the shoulders, digging his fingers into leather, muscle and bone. His fetid breath cupped Marc's mouth and nose, reminding him of unwashed animal and sour garbage. Marc clamped his mouth shut - felt another crunch, this time definitely a tooth - and tried to look away, only to see Zhao sliding his thumb back and forth between his fangs.

Zhen spun Marc around and slammed him hard against the opposite side of the alley. His jacket absorbed little of the impact. "You useless bag of flesh," Zhen snarled, his eyes reddening as he moved closer to Marc's throat. Marc thought to spit - he had plenty of spit left, and he might be able to loosen that tooth for extra impact - but giving these vampires even just a few drops of his bodily fluids could give them an extra boost of strength. Deciding he was already outmatched enough strength-wise, Marc simply glared at Zhen.

"Is that all you have?" Marc asked, and he couldn't help it. Flecks of blood sprayed from his split lips.

Zhen growled and lifted Marc, scraping his back up against the brick. Marc felt his feet leave the ground. His bloody-muddy brown hair strung loose around Marc's face. A low growling, like a sadistic purr, rolled from Zhen's throat. Marc tucked his chin to his chest as the undead Chinese twin pulled him closer.

"I can't imagine I'll find much satisfaction in the taste. But the thrill of watching you twitch will make up for it."

Zhen jerked Marc forward and shook him hard. Marc could no longer hold his head down; his chin lifted dangerously, exposing his throat.

When Zhen saw the thick black lines of a cross drawn on either side of Marc's neck, the purrs died. Zhen's hungry eyes widened when

Marc kicked him in the groin.

Zhao turned toward his brother while Marc crouched. Rolling behind Zhen, Marc kicked, aiming just behind his knee, but missed when Zhen recovered too quickly and pivoted to face Marc. Zhen started purring again, and Zhao, foregoing subtlety, started growling loudly.

Marc half-crawled, half-ran from the two vampires, heading back to the city street. He heard Zhao and Zhen chasing after him, their strides landing solidly on pavement. Just above him, to his left, Marc caught a glimpse of a rickety fire escape. Not wanting to have these vampires loose on the city streets, he leapt for the ladder. The lowest of the rusted rungs dug into his stomach as he pulled himself up and away.

"Where do you go now, Mr. Temple?" called Zhen. A few stories up, Marc stole a look down and behind him; both vampires were watching him as he scrambled up the side of the building. "Wherever you go, we will follow!"

It looked as if Zhen was sinking into the ground. Instead, he was preparing to jump, and with a powerful spring, he leapt to the second landing of the fire escape. The metal clanged down the alley and back again.

Marc saw Zhao preparing to leap, but didn't stay to watch. He turned and continued up the metal stairs of the crisscrossing fire escape. The undead pursuit stomped behind him as he scrambled to the rooftop.

Marc crested the roof. Light filtered up from the streets below, surrounding the rooftop playing field with a dull baleful glow. In the distance, Marc could hear cars and car radios, a motorcycle, the monorail, and, much closer, Zhen's perverse purring.

The vampire landed with a thud in front of Marc, having leapt the rest of the way up the building.

"I can't keep you two straight." The words slipped out of his mouth as Marc caught his breath. "Are you the one I already shot?"

Zhen charged at Marc, his fingers talonned at him. His jaw stretched open and unhinged, and he screamed, drowning the purr from his throat. The sound nearly overwhelmed Marc; he could barely hear the other vampire still jumping up the fire escape. His ears clogged, and his head felt lined with moss. Zhen ran straight for Marc, his arms outstretched and ready to grab the man standing before him.

Marc's equilibrium swirled. His knees finally gave out and he fell when Zhen should have been upon him.

Zhen tripped over Marc's crumpled body and disappeared over the side of the building.

The screaming stopped when the vampire hit the first landing of the fire escape. Zhao shouted something in Chinese, and there were more rusty thumps before Marc heard Zhen finally hit the ground.

Before getting to his feet, Marc fumbled at his right foot. Yanking his pant leg up, he pulled the single-shot Derringer from his ankle holster.

Marc turned and stood as an angered Zhao stepped to the roof. "Really, Mr. Temple. Another gun?"

He kept his grip firm on the small gun when Zhao backhanded him and sent him sprawling. The rooftop was gritty with smears of dirt and mud, and patches of small stones. A shopping cart missing two wheels lay on its side (how did that get up here?) in the near-center of the rooftop, and other garbage and debris peppered the area. Marc landed shoulder-first near a long dead body of a bird, its particular breed rendered unidentifiable long ago. Beyond it, a skylight struggled to reflect whatever moonlight made its way through the night sky.

Marc groaned and sat up as Zhao stalked him. He still held the Derringer, but he only had one shot. He had to make that one shot count, and he knew shooting at the vampire wildly wasn't an option.

So he turned and ran.

And stopped when he saw Zhen pulling himself over the ledge. The vampire's lower jaw hung loose, still distended, his fangs gleaming. Streaks of the vampire's blood trailed from one of his ears and already-healed scratches along his face. He lifted his arms in front of him, and with a soggy crunch, pushed the fingers of his right hand back into their sockets.

"You're just making us hungry, Mr. Temple," dripped Zhao from behind him. Marc cast a quick glance over his shoulder. The twin positioned himself behind Marc, creating a line between himself and his brother, making Marc a human point in between.

Zhen's growling tore through the night. Even from where he stood, Marc could smell that foul breath, and tightened his grip on the Derringer.

Following the two vampires into an unfamiliar alley was a mistake. He knew better, but he let his client's frantic phone call irritate him into carelessness. He had no stake. No holy water. He Sharpie'ed the crosses on his neck this morning out of habit.

Two hours ago, Marc was putting too much ketchup on a side of fries at the diner across the street from the cheap hotel he chose as his base of operations while in Seattle. The rest of his dinner was already cold when it was shoved in front of him by a waitress that didn't make eye contact. That was the reason he chose this diner and this part of town - no one seemed to pay too much attention. He didn't want to be remembered as having been here, or anywhere, for that matter.

When his cell phone buzzed in his jacket pocket, he dropped some bills on the table, and made for the door, careful not to appear too hurried or important enough to pay attention to.

Another call buzzed his phone before he was at least a block away from the diner; Marc wanted to be further away before picking up, so he let this one go to voicemail, too. He intended to listen to the messages once he was a comfortable distance from the diner, but a third call rang the phone. The caller ID showed all the calls all came from the same number.

The number he used to call his client when he first got to town.

"This is Temple." Marc kept walking, putting more distance between himself and his hotel.

"I found 'im. Yessir, I did."

Marc ignored the man wearing a worn jacket and face asking for money, making sure not to step into the puddle spreading beneath the man's mismatched shoes. "We were going to talk about this tomorrow."

"That's what y'said, but he's got himself a girl tonight."

Marc's pace slowed, and when he came to the crosswalk, he stopped completely and closed his eyes. What he did, he did for money, but this changed things. "How do you know?"

"It's my cousin. Well, second cousin. She went out lookin' for the vamp herself."

Marc fought the temptation to ask his client why he had someone else working his case. He worked alone.

He didn't need the liability, but his client gave him one anyway.

"I'm going to skip the part where I ask you why she was involved in my job and just ask you where she is now."

He gave Marc an address. A glance at a nearby street sign told Marc it was nearby. A few blocks at most. Convenient.

And something that should have tipped Marc off.

"We'll talk about how this changes my rate later." He crammed the phone back into his pocket. He was at least as far away from the hotel as he was from this supposed vampire and his hostage, so he chose to check it out first. He could always come back for his tools later if need be.

He didn't expect two vampires to be waiting for him.

"We would be disappointed if you took the easy way out, Mr. Temple." Zhen pressed a finger against the side of his head, pulled his thumb back and brought it down with a snap.

"At least, we hope you don't." Marc heard Zhao's feet shift behind him. "Drop the gun."

Marc braced himself when Zhen pulled his shoulders back, bunched his legs beneath him, and he leapt. He pointed the Derringer at the vampire, considered his best shot, and squeezed the trigger.

Zhen caught the bullet in his chest, turned to a halt, and smiled when Zhao's arms wrapped themselves around Marc's neck from behind.

"Looks like you'll be feeding my brother first." At some point, Zhen's growl turned to a low laugh. Marc tried to pull away.

He knew he'd put himself in this situation. It was his own fault, but if he did make it through the night, he knew he'd be charging his client a lot more than they'd originally discussed.

Zhao took a few steps forward, pushing Marc ahead of him. Zhen moved toward them, crushing the corpse of that bird underfoot.

Marc thought to pray.

Zhao stopped, holding Marc fast. "Do you hear that?"

Zhen stifled his hungry laughter and cocked his head.

Marc heard nothing out of the ordinary.

Zhao's breath moved from one side of the back of Marc's neck to the other. "A siren. It's getting closer."

"I don't hear it, brother."

"Neither do I." Marc tried to bring the vampires' attention back to himself. If the police were coming, keeping the vampires focused on him was the only thing he could do to help them.

"They're getting closer." Zhao shoved Marc to the side.

Marc's feet tangled themselves, and he turned just in time to avoid going face first through the skylight window.

Shards of glass, gravel and litter fell with him as he dropped into the space waiting below. He had a fleeting moment to cradle his head, and before closing his eyes, he saw the two vampires glaring down at him from the skylight. Zhao may have been smiling. Zhen was not.

With a wet slap, his world came to a softer stop than he expected. Opening his eyes, he found that he had landed on a dirty mattress. It was soaked with what he hoped was old rainwater from above. The vampires still stood above him, their attention on each other. He couldn't hear what they were saying over the sound of his thumping heartbeat in his ears, but that they weren't looking at him right now was enough. Marc stretched his legs slowly, and allowed himself a quick sigh of relief when he found he could still feel and move his toes. He wiggled his fingers and found the same.

The vampires were clearly arguing. Marc spread his arms from his sides, sliding them through standing water. His left arm was sore, but he found he could move it. With his right arm, he found hope.

Alongside the mattress, Marc touched something he'd used several times in his career, both as a government worker and as an independent contractor. It, too, was wet, and felt comfortable in his palm as he wrapped his fingers around it. He could feel the grain of it through its cheap veneer. Was it a broom? A mop? He remembered the time he destroyed a vampire with a plunger. He still lay flat on the mattress, but he lifted this wooden handle barely off the floor, getting a feel for its weight, guessing its length, and hoping for the best.

Looking at the vampires' silhouettes, Marc lost track of which vampire was which. They were still arguing, one flapping his arms in the others' direction. He could make out some of their words now, and if he spoke Chinese, he might have understood them.

"Hey!"

The Chinese stopped.

"Is that all you got?"

The room went black when the vampires jumped through the skylight, blocking out the stars. Marc tried to remember how long it took him to fall the distance, waited, dreading the hissing hot breath of the vampire leaping down at him, and at what he hoped was the right moment, pulled the wooden dowel in front of him.

A hiss turned to a growl then to a sigh. Marc felt the weight of the vampire crumple around the makeshift stake, gravity and the creature's own momentum pushing it down on its own destruction. This close, Marc recognized Zhen as the creature starting to claw at the wood, but strangely, every time his fingers touched it, he flinched back.

As Zhen flinched and twitched, Marc rolled the two of them over. When Zhen touched the mattress, he arched his back and screamed. There were words in the vampire's pain, but, again, they were in Chinese.

Finally trying to stand after he himself came through the skylight, Marc was surprised to find himself as uninjured as he was. He knew he'd be sore tomorrow, but he was certainly in better shape than the writhing corpse on the mattress.

Marc looked up. Zhao wasn't there.

His cellphone vibrated in his pocket.

While he was surprised the cell phone still worked, he wasn't taking any calls right now. He turned it off.

"Well done, Mr. Temple."

Marc tensed and glanced around the room, sliding the phone back into his soggy pocket, trying to find the source of Zhao's voice. His eyes were accustomed to the dark, but with every turn of his head, his blood pounded through his head.

"Where's the girl?"

"What girl?" Zhao was moving. "Oh, you mean my cousin." The pitch of Zhao's voice changed. "I mean, my second cousin."

Marc took a tentative step back toward what he hoped was a wall.

"There's no girl, Mr. Temple. No second cousin. And no police, either. But you're figuring that out now, right?"

Light flooded the room. Zhao stood near a light switch along the wall Marc was backing toward. While his eyes adjusted, he tried to focus on the vampire, slowly turning to face him. He knew he was weaponless again.

Or expected to be.

Zhen's corpse twitched under the fluorescents. Where his hands and face had touched the mattress, Marc could make out burns. The dead vampire seemed somehow weaker, his body losing shape. He lay on his side, his face beginning to melt.

"You've done me a great favor here, Mr. Temple."

"I don't do favors. I charge for my services."

Zhao laughed. "You expect me to pay you?"

Marc straightened his shoulders. "I did your job, didn't I?"

Zhao's laughter died in the space between vampire and human. "You're serious. I don't know if it's an American trait or a human trait, but your entitled nature is amusing."

Marc took a step toward Zhao, his wet feet splattering as he walked. "I'm not joking. You contacted me. You contracted me."

"Paying you would be pointless, Mr. Temple. You won't be leaving this warehouse. You'll die at the hands of the vampire whose brother you destroyed."

"Is that so?"

"No one will know I left you the tools to perform such a heinous act. Others will be told you set up this warehouse to ambush my brother, to kill him with that stake."

"The mattress?"

"I left it for you. You needed to be alive long enough to do your job."

"Holy water on the bed?"

"Extra insurance. But enough - this story ends with me being the one who stopped you."

"You'll be the one who set me up."

"I'll be the one who killed the man responsible for . . . oh, never mind." Zhao pushed off the wall, his arms stretching in front of him, his jaw dropping open.

Vampire hit human. The two folded into a ball and slid along the floor. Zhao screamed, his jaw snapped shut and when the water soaking Marc's jacket splashed in the vampire's face, Zhao flinched. Marc strained to lock his fingers behind Zhao's back and forced himself up, dragging the vampire with him.

Zhao struggled against the Holy water-doused human. He clawed at Marc. When Zhao caught a glance of the crosses on Marc's neck, he kicked at him. Marc struggled to keep his footing, and finally dragged Zhao the mattress. He tightened his arms, and hugged Zhao close to him before kicking Zhen's body to its side. Dead Zhen offered no resistance, and Marc pushed him over to kickstand the stake.

With a heave, Marc slammed Zhao onto it.

A wave of rancid steam pushed Marc off his feet. He gasped and watched Zhao curl against his dead undead brother, the two vampires back to back on the soaked mattress.

"Don't call me again."

Marc waited a few minutes, gingerly reached between to two melting vampires to retrieve his Beretta, and then he limped out of the warehouse.

THE LAW

(Originally published in *Dark: A Horror Anthology*,
Apparatus Revolution, 2010)

Rain collected in the divots of Marc Temple's black leather jacket. His dark hair hung in streaks across his forehead and into his vision as his tight eyes dared the body before him to rise. For good measure, he flexed his trigger finger and another bullet lost itself in the rotting corpse's head.

The rain muffled the sound of the gunshot as well as the meager parking lot area lights' illumination. Marc let the muzzle of the Beretta cool before tucking it underneath his jacket and into the back of his jeans. His eyes drifted from the dead thing to the parking lot itself. He moved the hair out of his face and scanned the area. Three cars, one his. One truck. Two dumpsters. A few shopping carts. No movement. The rain blanketed the shopping center's lot. Still no movement.

Marc scraped his car keys off the wet asphalt and unlocked his car door. He tried to brush the collecting water off his sleeves and shoulders before sliding inside; his wet shoes squished against the floorboards. Starting the engine first, Marc retrieved his cell phone from the glovebox. The cell's screen was flashing, indicating a new voicemail.

Not waiting long enough to let the engine warm up, Marc turned on the heat anyway and brought the phone to his ear. He let his eyes drift across the parking lot through the rainriverred windshield while he listened to the message.

"I know you told me not to call you once you started," it began. Marc recognized the nasal sound of the man's voice immediately. "But I wanted to tell you something important."

Marc's jaw shifted as he ground his teeth. "I know you told me I shouldn't have," the voice continued, "but I called the police. I didn't know - "

Marc dropped the cell phone on the passenger seat and turned on his headlights. Foggy beams of light slammed the dumpsters several feet in front of his car. Marc turned his head and surveyed the parking lot. The same truck. The same shopping carts. Still no movement. The two other cars . . .

Marc pushed on the gear shift and slowly backed out of the parking space. He turned the steering wheel, sweeping the blurred streaks of light across the lot. He drifted as the haloed headlights came across one of the cars. Through the wet darkness, he could make out details he missed before - a broken window, jagged scraps of torn fabric draped across the car door, the rain mixing with something darker, trailing away from the car.

And a dashboard police light hanging across the back of the driver's seat.

He reached behind, retrieved his Beretta and checked the ammunition. Half a clip. Marc punched off the phone before shifting the car back into "Park" and getting out.

He left the car door open as he inched his way toward the police car. The rain had let up just slightly. Marc moved toward the car alongside one of the fuzzy bright shafts of car headlight, his outstretched arm and gun carving a slice of shadow. He could see even more detail now - red mixed with the rain around the police car. Speckles of glass shimmered like tiny red rubies in the muted light of the parking lot. And blood.

Marc shook his head. He had been hired to take care of two of these things. Animated corpses, zombies, undead, whatever the client wanted to call them - he was paid good money to deal with two of them. Two. He put one down in the alley on the other side of the closed grocery store. That one was easy; it had no idea it was being hunted. The second one took Marc Temple by surprise. Attacking from underneath his car and moving faster than Marc would have liked, it tried to knock his gun from his hand, but only succeeded in making him drop his keys before catching the first of two bullets in the brain.

The brain was the key. For whatever reason, the zombie movies had it right. Those in Marc's profession had even jokingly named it "Romero's Law" after the director who made a number of the zombie films.

Marc watched for movement, but saw none. No more than a few feet away from the police car, he stopped his approach and started to circle the vehicle, keeping a slight distance between himself and anywhere one of those things could be hiding.

A thump. A scrape. Marc peered into the car, but saw nothing. The thumping noise again. The sound wasn't coming from inside the car.

The headlights of his own car were trying to reach him, but the moisture in the air and the police vehicle blocked them. The lights were shining directly at him, and that's where the sound came from.

With one hand, he brushed his hair out of his face, and with the other, he raised the gun. From the direction of his own car, another scraping sound, like wet wood on metal, sifted through the rain. Keeping the police car between himself and the source of the noise, Marc watched more intently, and saw movement.

It wasn't his car, but the dumpsters further behind it. Shadows gulped the light around them, and Marc could barely make out the figure - the partial figure - trying to pull itself out of the rusty green metal box.

Marc moved quickly to his own car and reached underneath the driver's seat. He pulled a flashlight and shot the beam at the dumpster. One half-hand had broken itself on the lip of the dumpster and the other hand had managed to wrap its rotten fingers around its edge. The top of the thing's head bobbed up-and-down as it tried to pull its wet, worm-eaten weight out of the dumpster.

Using the flashlight to mark his target, Marc took aim and waited for the head to raise high enough for him to get a good shot. It would only take one, but if there was an officer down, someone would eventually come looking for the missing policeman and he didn't want to be here when they came around. He had to do this quick and get out of this town, preferably tonight.

The flashlight's beam caught the gleaming near-triangle of skull white surrounded by a scabbed scalp and runny clumps of hair. Muddy eyes that had fallen deep into the thing's skull rolled loose as it finally brought its face to bear. Its features were slack and sanded away by decay. An ear - its left - hung limp, barely attached and resting on its shoulder.

Marc didn't hesitate. He pulled the trigger and the corpse's head burst into wet confetti.

As the loose body fell back into the confines of the dumpster, Marc heard more. He kept his flashlight and gun raised as he slowly advanced, straining his ears, ever listening for the inevitable sounds of police sirens. Through the rain, he heard it again. It wasn't the expected sirens. What he heard instead was a groan. Getting louder. Human? Coming from the dumpster.

Marc quickened his approach, his flashlight and gun barrel leading his eyes. He shot the flashlight beam into the dumpster, skimming over wet trash and garbage and two bodies. One was the creature he had already dispatched. The other was much more intact.

But not much. Half of his shirt had been torn, revealing equally torn and gnawed flesh beneath. Two circular chunks had been chewed away from the pale man's body - one from his neck and one from his arm. The flashlight reflected off the gold badge attached to the man's bloody belt. When Marc moved the light to the man's face, the light disappeared in another bite wound across the man's left cheek. The light pooled in his shocked pale brown eyes. He squinted and slowly moved his uninjured arm to block the light from his face.

Marc cast a quick look around, saw no further movement, and lowered his Beretta. "Can you stand?"

A shiver ran through the officer's body. "Maybe," slipped from his lips as he struggled to put his weight underneath him.

Marc took a few steps back. These walking dead didn't normally speak, but he didn't want to take any chances. He kept a finger wrapped around the trigger of his gun and watched as the policeman - a plain clothes officer - slumped over the edge of the dumpster and worked to put his feet solidly beneath him on the wet asphalt. His wounds were fresh. The rain washed a sheet of blood across his pallid face. "You have a license for that weapon?" The man's voice wobbled as much as his legs. An errant hand reached to the bite mark on his cheek.

Marc watched the policeman carefully. His gun was lowered, but he kept his finger arced around the trigger nonetheless. "How long?" he asked.

"What?"

"How long since you were bitten?"

"I don't . . . " His hand slumped to his side. "What time is it now?"

"Doesn't matter. You have a gun?"

"I did. I dropped it." He looked to the dumpster. "In there." He started to turn toward it.

The Beretta raised a few inches. "Leave it. You're going to need to listen to me, and I'm tired of getting rained on. Your car. Come on."

The officer hesitated until Marc raised the Beretta a few inches more. His hand trailing back to his chewed cheek, he slowly started back toward the police car. Marc glanced around the parking lot before following, watching, listening for more.

Rain found its way through the car's broken driver's side window, soaking the seat pink. The headrest had been torn off, and spongy stuffing oozed through the rips and tears in the seat itself. The wounded policeman slumped as Marc slid into the dryer passenger's seat. He kept the gun on the man as he pulled the door closed.

"I'm going to tell you some things, and I need you listen. To really listen. I don't want to hear, 'That's impossible,' or, 'You're crazy.'"

The policeman nodded.

"And I really don't want to hear, 'Dead things don't attack people.'"

The policeman blinked. Marc inhaled. "I'll give you the Reader's Digest version as we . . . " What was left of the man's collar had finally reached its saturation point and now blood from the man's neck wound was starting to drip down his chest. "You don't have much time."

"What do you mean?"

"You're going to die. Soon."

"So take me to a hospital. Please . . . "

Marc shook his head. "There's nothing that can be done. And even if there was . . . " He gestured the Beretta at the man's neck. "I couldn't get you there in time. Did you call for back-up?"

"What?"

"Before you came here. Did you call for back-up?"

The man hesitated. Marc's eyes tensed, urging for an answer. "No. I should have, but . . . No. I didn't. Artie called me on my way home, so I just thought I'd swing by."

Arthur Letzler was the name of the client.

Marc cast another survey around the parking lot. Still nothing. Back to the policeman.

"Family?"

"No. An older brother in Tulsa, but . . . no . . . no one." His voice was starting to waver. "I'm cold."

"Start the car and turn on the heat."

The police car's heater rattled lukewarm air at first, but slowly started warming.

"I'm going to die?"

"Yes. If it makes you feel any better, it's not your fault. If you're the kind of person that needs to blame others, blame Letzler. He had no business calling you after he hired me."

"Hired you?" Marc chose his next words carefully. "I handle 'special eliminations.' I'm an exterminator."

"The thing in the dumpster?"

"Right. Letzler only hired me for two, but it looks like a third got you. Did you see any more?"

The policeman shook his head. "I don't think so."

"When they bite you, you die. It might not happen right away, depending on the severity of the bite, but you will." He paused. "What's worse is that after you die, you eventually come back as one of them."

"Like in the movies?"

"Just about."

The policeman sighed. Over that sigh, the sound of the car engine and heater, Marc thought he heard something else. Another gasp?

"What are you going to do . . . to me?" The rain had started to come down hard again. Rain drops on the car's roof peppered the warming air with soft thuds. It was getting harder to hear much more than the car and the officer's own wet breathing.

"I haven't decided - "

A slimy sucking sound interrupted Marc. A splotched green-and-brown arm shot between the driver's and passenger's seat. If the window hadn't already been broken out, the policeman would have slammed his head against the glass as he jumped in surprise. Marc twisted and saw the undead clawing its way up from the floor between the front and back seats. It had been younger - a pre-teen girl - in life, and its hungry eyes stared into him. The girl's tee-shirt was splattered with dripping mud and several maggoty worms clung to one of her armpits. Her face twisted in what looked like a combination of desire, pain and rage.

"Get her off me! Get it off me!"

The girl's eyes were on Marc, but its arms and searching fingers had found the policeman. Her right hand snaked its way around his seat and her crusty fingernails were tearing at the bite wound in his cheek. He tried to turn away from her, and lunged forward. He jerked, and into Marc's raising arm, knocking the Beretta away and to the floor.

The girl-thing hurked over the seat, crawling toward the two men. The policeman writhed and coiled away from her as best he could. Marc reached out and tried to move her head away from the two of them, lifting her face (careful to keep his fingers away from her teeth) to the roof. He pushed until a wet vegetable-cracking sound vibrated through her neck as Marc cracked dead vertebrate with a shove.

Her body spasmed, but her weight kept coming after the policeman. Marc reached to the wet floorboards, his fingers searching for his gun. The tips of his index and middle finger skimmed the grip of it. He would have to release his hold on the girl's head to reach it. Cold drool dribbled down her cheek and iced itself down Marc's arm and into his coat sleeve. He shoved her away and bent to retrieve the weapon.

As he brought it to bear, the policeman shifted the car from 'Park' to 'Drive.'

The dying man stomped on the accelerator. Wet tires took hold, heaving the policeman's car across the asphalt. The dead girl slipped into the back seat, taking a few fresh inches of the policeman's face under her fingernails. He screamed while Marc tried to take aim, but the policeman jerked the steering wheel and all three bodies lunged to the side.

The vehicle slid around the parking lot, narrowly missing one of the other cars. Through the diffusing rain, Marc watched his car speed by as well. The policeman was still accelerating, but he was avoiding the other vehicles in the lot, leaving them behind.

The girl flung herself between the two front seats. Her right arm flipped across Marc's shoulder, knocking back his Beretta and sending a burst of collected rain water flying from his jacket. Her loosely-held head landed on the policeman's thigh. With a wet gurgle, she/it opened her jaw as wide as she could and started tearing through his pants with her teeth. Her left arm pushed at his face.

The policeman's screams turned to sobs until some of her teeth found their way through to his flesh, then he screamed again. Marc tightened the grip on his handgun and slammed the barrel against the girl's skull, but he couldn't find an angle that wouldn't send the bullet through its dead head but into the policeman's groin as well.

The policeman stopped turning the wheel. Marc looked up to see him opening his mouth wide, bearing his teeth as the screaming drifted into breathy laughter. He held the wheel steady; rain splattered in through his broken window. The girl continued to chew on his leg.

Marc cast a quick glance through the windshield. The speeding car was pointed at the dumpster.

"What are you - " The question died before it left his lips. As the policeman's eyes grew wider and tears leaked down his cheeks, Marc pushed the girl's arm away from him and turned to reach for his door handle. His damp fingers slid against the chrome-plated lever, but he eventually found purchase and, snagging a fingernail, managed to pop it open.

The car continued to race toward the dumpster. Marc cast one last look at the terrified policeman before shoving the door open and spilling himself out on the asphalt.

His body rolled in a controlled crumple, coming to a stop in time for Marc to watch the policeman's car hurtle into the dumpster. Metal squealed and tires spun. Through the misted light, Marc could barely see the policeman convulsing in the driver's seat. The rear wheels kept pushing the car into the metal dumpster. Rain mixed with the rapidly spilling dark fluids coming from the car's undercarriage. Above the noise and the rain, Marc could hear the screaming laughter from the victim of his client's mistake. The laughter died beneath a whooshing sound as something sparked and caught fire. The pooling liquid around the crashed car lit with light blue flame. Marc threw a hand up to cover his eyes as the car burst into fire. A quick gush of heat flicked over him.

Marc slowly came to his feet, noting a stiff pain in his left leg and ankle. He limped to his own car while wiping the Beretta off as much as he could on his pants. He tossed the weapon inside before easing himself into the car. The seat was soaked and oozed rain water as he let his weight settle into it.

The blazing police car and dumpster proved to be a greater force than the rain and licked the night air with feathers of flame. Marc pulled his car door closed and exhaled. The engine was still running. The heater was still on, and it was warm.

The phone rang. Marc stared at his cell phone for a moment before grabbing it, his eyes focusing on it. He picked it up and held it to his face.

"Yeah."

The nasal voice on the other end sounded surprised. "Mr. Temple?"

"Yeah." Marc could hear the man breathing obnoxiously loud.

"I thought . . . I was expecting - "

"What do you want, Arthur?"

"Did the police . . . ? I mean, I called the police."

Marc slid his car into gear. He rolled down his window as the car inched toward the burning police car. "I know you did, Arthur. I got your message."

"Oh. Right." He paused and breathed into the phone. "Did they get in the way?"

Marc steered the car away from the fire, passing it on his left. He peered into the flames as best he could, squinting. No movement.

"Your police friend's dead now, Arthur, but no, he didn't really get in the way."

Before waiting for his client's response, Marc tossed the cell phone out the window and into the fire before driving off.

ABOUT THE AUTHOR

Some say Derek M. Koch was born 30 years too late. Some say he spends too much time watching classic monster movie trailers on YouTube. And some just want him to take off his luchador mask and stop writing about fighting monsters.

Derek is the creator of the *Supernatural Solutions: The Marc Temple Casefiles* series, as well as the upcoming *6-Week Rotation* series of superhero novels. When not writing, Derek is producing the award-winning Monster Kid Radio podcast, the weekly podcast celebrating the classic, and sometimes not-so-classic, genre cinema of yesteryear

When not online, he can be found at home in the Pacific Northwest with his cat, his luchador masks, and his funny-shaped dice.

Find Derek online at http://linktr.ee/itspronouncedcook

Made in the USA
Las Vegas, NV
08 February 2023

67154587R00049